Henry Cecil was the [ ] Leon. He was born i. [...] Green Rectory, near London, England in 1902. He studied at Cambridge where he edited an undergraduate magazine and wrote a Footlights May Week production. Called to the bar in 1923, he served with the British Army during the Second World War. While in the Middle East with his battalion he used to entertain the troops with a serial story each evening. This formed the basis of his first book, *Full Circle*. He was appointed a County Court Judge in 1949 and held that position until 1967. The law and the circumstances which surround it were the source of his many novels, plays, and short stories. His books are works of great comic genius with unpredictable twists of plot which highlight the often absurd workings of the English legal system. He died in 1976.

BY THE SAME AUTHOR
ALL PUBLISHED BY HOUSE OF STRATUS

THE
PAINSWICK LINE

by

Henry Cecil

This edition published in 2000 by House of Stratus, an imprint of
Stratus Books Ltd., 21 Beeching Park, Kelly Bray,
Cornwall, PL17 8QS, UK.

www.houseofstratus.com

A catalogue record for this book is available from the British Library
and the Library of Congress.

ISBN 1-84232-061-0

Contents

CHAPTER ONE

Court Selection

It would surprise many people to learn that a judge of the High Court of Justice had ever asked a clergyman of the Church of England what horse he fancied for the 2.30 on the following day. Still, it is not absolutely impossible, though it is most improbable, that such a question has been asked informally by the one of the other on a very few occasions. It must, however, be unique in the annals of legal history to find this question being asked by the judge from the bench of the clergyman as a witness. That, in fact, is what happened in Court 1 of the Old Bailey during the hearing of the case of *Rex v Smith*. If you could obtain access to the shorthand note of Lucy Meeson-Smith's trial, you would find there recorded:

THE JUDGE: Surely this matter is capable of reasonable proof one way or the other. What do you say will win the 2.30 race tomorrow?

THE WITNESS: I am afraid I cannot tell your Lordship that, as I have not considered the race and, indeed, even if I had considered it, I might not be able to give the answer. There are many races of which I could not hope to find the winner except by luck.

1

THE JUDGE: That, I suppose, is the experience of most people with all races. Is there any race of which you can tell us the winner with reasonable certainty? Any race in the future, I mean.

THE WITNESS: Oh, yes, my Lord.

THE JUDGE: Tell us, then. No doubt the jury will make a note of your answer and profit by the information – or not – as the case may be.

THE WITNESS: My Lord, the Oaks will unquestionably be won by Sonata, and the Derby will almost as certainly be won by Intermezzo. I must make one qualification. Sonata has once been known to refuse to start. Of course, if she refuses again, my forecast will be wrong, but, if she starts, she will win.

THE JUDGE: Do these horses happen to be favourites for the respective races?

THE WITNESS: No, my Lord. At the moment the favourite for the Oaks is My Conscience and the betting on it is 2 to 1 against. Your Lordship could obtain 12 to 1 against Sonata. Your Lordship will forgive me; I was not intending to be personal. Intermezzo is at present at 20 to 1, while the favourite Umbrella is at 3 to 1. So the double on Sonata and Intermezzo is worth 240 to 1. It should be 272 to 1, but no bookmaker will lay the odds.

THE JUDGE: I'm not sure that I understand your last remark, but never mind about that for the moment. When are these races being run?

THE WITNESS: The Oaks is on Thursday and the Derby on Saturday.

THE JUDGE: Very well then. Subject to anything which may be said by counsel on either side, I shall adjourn this trial until Monday next.

MR TRUMPER: Does your Lordship think a forecast of two races is sufficient? The witness might be lucky.

THE JUDGE: Well, Mr Meeson-Smith, you hear what counsel says. Can you make any other forecasts for races this week?

THE WITNESS: (*after a pause*): Yes, my Lord. Gorgonzola will win the Royal Stakes Handicap on Friday, and I shall be very surprised if Chirrup doesn't win the first race at Epsom on Saturday.

THE JUDGE: At what price do these horses stand?

THE WITNESS: There is no betting on them yet, my Lord. The races are not big races and there is no ante-post betting, as it is called, on them. I should, however, anticipate that Gorgonzola will run as a complete outsider, while Chirrup should be third or fourth favourite. I must, however, make another qualification. Those horses are likely to win if they run, but naturally I cannot tell if the owners and trainers will run them.

THE JUDGE: Well, Mr Trumper, are four enough for you?

MR TRUMPER: Yes, I think so, my Lord – if they run.

THE JUDGE: Very well then. I take it, Mr Croft, you have no objection to this adjournment.

MR CROFT: None at all, my Lord, I welcome it.

THE JUDGE: Members of the jury, I am proposing to adjourn this trial until Monday to see whether the witness's prophecies turn out to be accurate. Don't talk about the case during the adjournment or try to come to any conclusion about it. You haven't yet heard the whole of the evidence. Whether or not you avail yourselves of Mr Meeson-Smith's hints is entirely a matter for you.

Adjourned until Monday, the 7th June, at 10.30 a.m.

In order to explain how such matters came to be considered in a Court of law, and a Criminal Court at that, it is necessary to go back some years and to trace the history of Lucy Meeson-Smith and her father, the Reverend Wellsby Meeson-Smith, from the time of her innocent childhood to the day when she came to stand in the dock at the Old Bailey. It can, however, be said at once that all four horses won at odds which were highly satisfactory from the point of view of those who backed them.

Lucy Meeson-Smith was the Reverend Wellsby Meeson-Smith's only child. He was thirty when he married and his wife twenty, and it was shortly after he obtained the living at Tapworth Magna that Lucy was born. She was an attractive girl of a most enquiring turn of mind and she had difficulty in accepting anything which was not satisfactorily proved before her eyes. Her father had read Mathematics at Cambridge, and it may be that this trait was to some extent inherited from him. He delighted to play with figures, but, while she was more interested in less concrete matters, she required the same certainty as can be obtained with figures. She quickly learned that two and two made four, and seeing this clearly proved by the use of bricks in the nursery, she required the same standard of proof for the theory of the Universe. This her father and mother and teachers were wholly unable to provide. As she grew up she asked more and more awkward questions and received what she considered to be wholly unsatisfactory answers. At the age of thirteen, for instance, she asked her teacher to explain how it came about that the Almighty permitted cruelty to animals. She could, even at that age, understand the explanation given to her for the misery of many apparently deserving human beings. Man has to work out his salvation, she was told, the ways of God are inscrutable and mankind as a whole must go through the refining process which involves apparent unfairness to worthy individuals. She accepted the story of Job and, indeed, most of the cruelties revealed

4

in the Old Testament, provided that men or women were the sufferers. The proposed sacrifice of Isaac – particularly as it was never carried out – she found easy to understand, but the ram caught in a thicket, which was slaughtered instead of Isaac, brought her to tears. 'Poor ram,' she used to say, 'poor, poor ram. Why did it have to be killed, please? What had it done?' 'They were primitive men in those days and did barbarous things,' she was told; 'we know better today.' 'Does God approve of rabbits being caught in traps, then?' she would ask. 'Why does He allow it?' 'Now, don't ask so many questions,' she was told. Indeed, this seemed the only answer to many of her queries.

'Is it good to be kind to animals?' she asked at Sunday School one day.

'Yes, of course, Lucy.'

'Do caterpillars feel pain if they are stamped on?'

'Perhaps.'

'If they are left in the road will they be stamped on?'

'Probably.'

'I was picking them up and putting them on the side of the road when Daddy told me that we'd be late for church if I went on doing that, and that my hands would be all dirty.'

'Your father knows best.'

'Does God like caterpillars to be stamped on, then?'

'Don't ask so many questions.'

But although Lucy would sometimes stop asking, she did not stop thinking, and she returned to the subject time after time.

'If animals have souls, why do we eat them and why can't they come to church? If they haven't souls, why does God let millions and millions of them die in torture every day? Why does He let the spider catch the fly in its web?

Does He see it struggling? Doesn't He mind? And if He does why doesn't He do something about it?'

When she was fifteen she drew a picture of a cat about to kill a bird. She took considerable trouble over it and the look of cruel greed on the cat's face and the sweet innocence of the bird were well depicted. In a corner of the picture was a similar bird calmly eating a worm which was wriggling in its beak. She gave the picture the title 'God is Love.' That was the only time she saw her father really angry. He tore up the picture and said she was a very wicked little girl. 'For thinking of the picture or the title?' she asked. 'For blasphemy,' he said. 'Do you think God likes such things?' 'Then why doesn't He stop them?' she asked. 'Never let me see you do that again,' said her father, and walked away.

She was kind and generous and she could not believe that an almighty power, full of loving kindness, could permit animals to suffer as they do. Religion, therefore, meant little to her. Still, while she lived at home, she went to church and did all the things which the well-behaved daughter of a good vicar is expected to do. After a normal schooling, she took a secretarial course and eventually went to live in London on her own. Her parents were not at first happy about this, but there was nothing they could do to stop her and, as she used to stay with them for weekends and appeared to be coming to no harm, they eventually accepted the position. She took various jobs, picking and choosing as young ladies with Mrs Blankworthy's certificate of efficiency always can. Some months before her trial she became employed by Vulgan's, the big bookmakers. She chose the job because it was well paid and because she wanted to know what the inside of a bookmaker's office was like. Her eventual prosecution at the Old Bailey arose from her employment there. She was employed as a clerk in the telephone room and among her duties was that of taking bets from the numerous clients of Messrs Vulgan who made their bets by telephone. She was, of course, one of many, and it was some time before the security department of her employers became interested in her. One day, however, the manager asked one of the security men to keep a watch on Miss Smith. (When applying for jobs she had dropped the Meeson as rather cumbersome.) The manager had noticed that a certain Mr Thompson, whose account had been dormant for a considerable time, had suddenly changed his address and started operating again with singular success. Messrs Vulgan were perfectly happy to pay out genuine winners; it did their business good by way of advertisement and, in any event, there were so few of them, compared with the number of losers, that they could well afford it. Not unnaturally, however, they had a serious objection to being cheated, and since a regular backer of horses, in spite of occasional runs of good luck, is usually a loser, repeated and consistent wins excite suspicion. The manager, noticing that Mr Thompson seemed to be winning too often, investigated his account and found to his astonishment that for the past three months he had rarely lost a bet. He did not bet in large amounts and the loss was nothing to Vulgan's, but the consistency of the wins called for investigation. This revealed that the bets were always taken by Lucy Smith. That was certainly strange, as the chances of a client being put through to the same clerk each time were very small indeed in view of the number employed. Accordingly, Mr Grant, a member of the security department, interviewed Lucy.

'We've noticed,' he said, 'that Mr Henry Thompson of 11 Pocket Lane, Streatham, is winning nearly all his bets.'

'Nice for him,' said Lucy.

7

'Very,' said Mr Grant. 'Not a friend of yours, I suppose?'

'Wish he were.'

'Not a relative, I suppose? You know the rule about servants of the Company and their relatives not being accepted as clients.'

'Yes, of course.'

'We've also noticed,' said Mr Grant, 'that you seem to take all his bets.'

'I must bring him luck.'

'Sure there's nothing you'd like to tell me about him?'

'Nothing at all, but I'd like to know why you're asking me all these questions.'

'Just a routine check up. We always keep an eye on winning accounts.'

'That should be easy.'

The interview ended and Lucy went back to her work.

That evening, when Lucy with some misgivings called at 11 Pocket Lane to collect the money due from Vulgan's to Mr Thompson for the previous week's winnings, she was not pleased to find Mr Grant waiting for her.

'Well,' said Mr Grant, 'it was easy, as you said.'

'I can explain,' said Lucy.

'You need to,' said Mr Grant.

'Mr Thompson is a friend of mine, but I didn't like to tell you before. I collect his letters for him.'

'Why does he use an accommodation address?'

'Why shouldn't he?'

'Where does he live then?'

'I'm not quite sure of his present address.'

'How will you give him the money? I notice he likes it to be in cash.'

'I shall see him some time.'

'Where?'

'Oh – somewhere or other.'

'When?'

'You do want to know a lot, don't you. Well, there isn't a Mr Thompson, anyway.'

'You surprise me,' said Mr Grant.

'I can explain,' said Lucy.

'Don't bother,' said Mr Grant. 'Keep it for the police. Your explanations bore me. They're too easy. I like something a bit meatier.'

'Oh, well, if you don't want to know,' said Lucy, 'that's your affair. Anyway, I'm resigning.'

'That's very decent of you. But you needn't bother. You're fired already.'

'You can't fire me.'

'The Company will as soon as they have my report. If I were you, young lady, I should take it a bit more seriously. This is a police matter.'

'I meant to ask you why you said that before. What have I done wrong?'

'Well, you are a cool one. You ask the magistrate. He'll tell you.'

'I certainly will. Where is he?'

'At Marlborough Street.'

'I'll go tomorrow.'

'Perhaps you will.'

'Who shall I ask for?'

'They'll tell you.'

'Who d'you mean by "they"?'

'Oh – you make me tired. See you in the morning. I shouldn't do a bunk. They'll find you and it only makes it worse. Good night.'

Some days later Lucy was called from her work to the manager's office.

'Sit down, Miss Smith, please,' he said. 'This is Sergeant Powell and this is Detective Holden of the Criminal

Investigation Department,' he added, indicating two strangers who were there with Mr Grant.

'How d'you do?' said Lucy.

'Miss Smith,' said the sergeant, 'I have a warrant for your arrest. Messrs Vulgan have charged you with obtaining from them £75 by false pretences with intent to defraud. I must warn you that anything you say will be taken down in writing and may be given in evidence.'

'What was the fraud? I won the money.'

'Now, Miss, it's no business of mine to advise you, but you're more likely to get off lightly if you make a clean breast of it. I don't suppose it's your fault. Who's the man behind you?'

'Mr Thompson of 11 Pocket Lane.'

'He doesn't exist.'

'I daresay, but he's the only man behind me.'

'Oh, very well, Miss, have it your own way, but don't say I didn't warn you. Now d'you want to state how you inserted the bets? You needn't if you don't want to.'

The manager looked at Lucy. This was the question he really wanted answered. They had what they thought was a foolproof system at Vulgan's, and none of them could think how Lucy could have broken it down. If she had only done it once, it would have been worrying enough, but that she had been able to do it for weeks, if not months, was a matter of great anxiety. If she could do it so easily, so could the others. The answer must be found. He had told the detective-sergeant that they would even be prepared to drop the charge if he could find out how she'd done it.

'Inserted the bets? What do you mean?'

'Now, look here,' said the sergeant, 'you don't have to say anything at all if you don't want to, but you know perfectly well those bets weren't on the level and, if you tell us how you did it, your employers may – I don't say they will – may drop the charge.'

'Of course they were on the level. What rubbish you talk.'

'Then why all the lies you told?'

'How could I put a bet on any other way?'

'Why not bet with someone else?'

'How could I know the runners? or jockeys? or the prices?'

'You can read the morning papers.'

'Read the morning papers. It's obvious you don't bet, Sergeant. What you see in the morning papers is what are called 'probables'. That doesn't mean runners. It means what it says. Probables. Some of them don't run and some improbables do. I can't learn that until half an hour before the race, and then I'm on duty. Then the jockeys are changed too, with a possible change of weights involved. Then what about the prices? The forecasts in the morning papers are hopeless. I don't back blindly like most of our clients. I want to know what I'm doing. The only way I could do it was by using a false name.'

'That's all very well,' said the manager, 'but how did you choose all those winners?'

'Yes, Miss,' added the sergeant, 'how did you do that?'

Lucy hesitated. Then, 'I won't tell you,' she said, 'I chose them and they won. That's enough for you.'

'It just about is,' said the manager. 'No one could do it.'

'Well, I did.'

'How?'

'That's my business.'

'Then it's our business if we choose to disbelieve you. All right, Sergeant, we'll proceed with the charge.' As Lucy said nothing to this, he added angrily: 'You're a very stupid young woman. If you'll tell us how you did it, we'll drop the whole thing.'

'Well, I won't. You just won't believe anyone can beat you, that's your trouble.'

'Nor will you, young lady, but you'll find you're mistaken.'

Nothing more was to be obtained from Lucy and she was accordingly taken to the police station, charged and then released on her own bail.

CHAPTER TWO

Bogg, Tewkesbury & Co.

The next day she appeared at Marlborough Street Police Court, where the magistrate asked her if she had any money and, on being told that she had a little, suggested that she should take legal advice and remanded her on bail for the purpose. In consequence she eventually found herself in the offices of Bogg, Tewkesbury & Co., solicitors and commissioners for oaths. After a few words with a pert young lady who might have filled any position in the firm from office girl to cashier (and, in fact, combined them all), Lucy was shown in to Mr Tewkesbury himself. As it was only eleven o'clock in the morning, Mr Tewkesbury did not reek of whisky. He merely exuded that unpleasant smell of the previous week's intake which Lucy, in her innocence, mistook for a lack of attention to his teeth.

'Good morning, young lady,' he said with half-closed eyes, and then, observing the form and fairness of Lucy, got up unsteadily and assisted her into a chair. She did not need the assistance, but Mr Tewkesbury, whose main pleasure in life was whisky, had not yet entirely lost other elementary feelings and liked touching pretty young women when he got the chance.

'Well, what can I have the pleasure of doing for you?'

'I'm in trouble.'

'Trouble, young lady, can be of many kinds. It can range from a badly wanted affiliation order to murder, though, if I may say so, from the look of you, I should not imagine you have come to consult me about either of these matters.'

'No.'

'Then perhaps you would enlighten me, and don't forget, time is money, and my time is represented by your money. Expensive business going to law. We take all your money, you know.' He smiled as pleasantly as nature allowed him.

'I'm charged with fraud.'

'Oh dear. I hoped it was shoplifting. So much cheaper. Expensive business fraud. How much money have you got?'

'Eight guineas.'

'Eight guineas? Dear, dear dear, that won't go very far. Can't instruct counsel on eight guineas, Sure you haven't any more?'

'None at all.'

'Can't you sell something?'

'No.'

'Oh, well, give me what you have and I'll do the best I can.'

'You want the money now?'

'Certainly, young lady. We're not like taxi-drivers who get paid at the end of the journey. Sometimes, you see, our clients disappear for a time at the end of the journey. But don't let's talk about unpleasant things. Eight guineas, I think you said. They'll give you a receipt in the office.'

Lucy counted out the money and handed it over.

'Thank you,' said Mr Tewkesbury. 'Now, when is the case coming on?'

'At Marlborough Street in a week's time.'

'Very well, I shall be there.' Mr Tewkesbury got up to indicate that the interview was closed.

'But don't you want to know about the case?'

'Plenty of time for that. A week you said, I think. I'll be outside the Court. Don't you worry. Leave it all to me.' He approached Lucy to assist her from the chair, but she was able to forestall him. He managed, however, to take her arm and hold it while he repeated: 'Don't you worry. Leave it to me,' and to retain his grip while he showed her to the door. Fortunately for her and unfortunately for him the distances in the offices of Bogg, Tewkesbury & Co. were extremely small, and it was not long before Lucy was in the street again. As soon as she had gone, Mr Tewkesbury's dying amatory instincts subsided and he sent for the pert young lady.

'Go round to Roebucks, please, Nora,' he said, handing her three pounds.

'Same as usual, Mr Tewkesbury?'

'Of course. Hurry up. I've a lot to do.'

He had, in fact, a certain amount to do, but the work he had in mind was the commencement of the day's drinking, which Lucy's eight guineas had conveniently accelerated.

It may surprise some people to know that there are firms like Bogg, Tewkesbury today, but, though there are very few of them, they have a real existence. Until they are actually proved to have misappropriated their clients' monies they continue, not necessarily to flourish, but certainly to carry on business, disapproved of most strongly by the Law Society but otherwise not interfered with. Those who have had the misfortune to get into trouble of one kind or another and to have had their troubles increased by consulting a firm of this type will recognise only too well Lucy's experiences already and to be related.

Lucy did not see Mr Tewkesbury again until just before the case was called on, when he walked unsteadily into the Court. He winked at Lucy, who was by that time in the dock, and sat down heavily at the solicitors' table.

As the evidence of each witness was taken, Mr Tewkesbury informed the magistrate that he would reserve cross-examination. After half an hour the case was adjourned for a further week. Lucy saw Mr Tewkesbury outside the Court. This time she could smell whisky quite distinctly.

'Don't you worry, young lady,' he said, somewhat thickly. 'It's going very nicely.'

'But you haven't heard my story yet.'

Mr Tewkesbury placed his finger against his nose, which, somewhat to his surprise, he had no difficulty in finding, and winked knowingly at Lucy.

'You leave it to me, young lady. You wait and see. You'll be surprised. See you next week,' and he lurched away.

Lucy had no experience of the law or lawyers, but she began to have misgivings. The next week the same performance was repeated and the case was again adjourned for a week. At the end of the third hearing the case for the prosecution was closed.

The case made against Lucy was that she was employed as a clerk to accept telephoned bets; that she placed bets in a false name knowing that she was not allowed to bet with her employers; that when tackled with this, she lied about it, and that she told further lies later on to Mr Grant. It was shown that she had backed an exceptional number of winners, and the evidence was, that no client of her employers had ever enjoyed such continuous success. There was no direct evidence that she had made the bets after the result of the race was known, but the magistrate was asked to infer this from the other facts.

Then Mr Tewkesbury rose unsteadily to his feet. 'I submit,' he said to the magistrate, 'that my client has no case to answer – no case at all.'

He sat down again heavily.

'Would you care to elaborate your submission, Mr Tewkesbury?' said the magistrate.

Mr Tewkesbury rose.

'Your Worship?' he said.

'Would you care to elaborate your submission?' repeated the magistrate.

'No case to answer,' said Mr. Tewkesbury. 'No case at all,' he repeated, and sat down.

'That isn't very helpful, Mr. Tewkesbury,' said the magistrate.

'Not helpful?' said Mr. Tewkesbury from where he sat. 'Never been told that before.'

The magistrate turned to the solicitor for the prosecution with a slight sigh. 'What evidence is there of intent to defraud, Mr Highly?' he asked. 'There's no direct evidence that the bets were placed after the races were over, is there?'

'No, your Worship, but I ask you to say that the defendant's conduct is only consistent with an intent to defraud, or, at any rate, that that is a question for the jury to decide.'

The magistrate hesitated. Finally, 'Yes,' he said. 'I think there is evidence to go before a jury.'

Lucy was accordingly committed to take her trial at the Old Bailey and was allowed bail as before. Outside the Court she saw Mr. Tewkesbury.

'Well, young lady,' he said, 'we had a good try. Too bad we didn't get away with it. Never mind. Better luck next time.'

'What will happen now?' said Lucy.

'First of all,' said Mr. Tewkesbury, 'I shall want some more money.'

'But I haven't any.'

Mr Tewkesbury winked. 'Find some.'

'But I can't.'

Mr Tewkesbury looked pained.

'But I can't do all this for nothing, you know. Not a charitable institution. You owe me five guineas already.'

'Five guineas? But I gave you eight.'

'All gone,' said Mr Tewkesbury. 'After all, I've appeared for you three times.'

'You haven't said very much.'

'It's quality,' said Mr Tewkesbury, 'not quantity, that counts. I could have said a great deal if I'd just been a windbag, but that wouldn't have done you any good. Well – well, can you find any more money, or can't you?'

'I can't.'

'In that case,' said Mr Tewkesbury, 'I'm afraid that I've done all I can for you. Very sorry, but not a charitable institution. Nice to have known you. Must be getting along now. You'll be all right, don't you worry. Send me the five guineas when you've got it. Good morning,' and Mr Tewkesbury walked out of Lucy's life.

CHAPTER THREE

A Glance at the Old Bailey

Lucy was now in a quandary. She had made up her mind that she would, if possible, prevent news of her prosecution from coming to the ears of her father. She hoped that, even if the case were reported, the name of Lucy Smith was so common that it would not attract his attention. She saw no reason whatever why he should be dragged into the proceedings, which would not only distress him but would undoubtedly cause gossip in the village. Now, however, that she had no legal adviser she did not quite know what to do. She was a resourceful young woman, however, and decided to go down to the Old Bailey to watch a trial so as to see whether she could conduct her own defence. So she went the next day, and watched for some hours from the public gallery. She was surprised to find that the people in the dock seemed far more respectable than her neighbours in the public gallery.

The first case which she saw was that of a handsome young man in a clean and well-pressed blue suit. Before the charge was read over to him, she wondered what it could be and imagined it must be some form of fraud. Next to her, on her right in the gallery, was a man who to her mind was an obvious burglar, while the man on her left was a gentleman with a receding forehead, near-set eyes, and a large ungainly body, who looked as though he were capable of committing any crime not requiring intelligence. Both these characters were so very different from the nice boy in the dock. To her amazement, however, when the charge was read out, she found that the nice boy was accused of robbery with violence; possessing house-breaking implements by night; and of larceny from a dwelling-house. She had yet to learn that the normal prisoner, particularly the man charged with crimes of violence, dresses himself as well as possible when standing his trial, while those who have already served their sentences go to the gallery, dressed in their everyday clothes, to observe with relish the same things happening to other people as happened to themselves.

The proceedings in the Court filled Lucy with awe, and she began to wonder how she would find her voice so as to enable her to put forward her defence. The judge in his imposing robes; the clerk and the bewigged barristers; the size of the Court; and the whole atmosphere made her feel very doubtful if she were capable of going through with it. She then realised with a sinking feeling that hers was no appointment that could be cancelled. It was while she was feeling in this mood that the trial of the handsome gentleman in the blue suit was postponed for a few minutes, while another gentleman was brought up from below. It appeared that the gentleman from below possessed £2 4s 6d and wished to have the services of learned counsel to defend him. The judge informed him of his right to choose any of the learned counsel sitting in Court.

Lucy had vaguely heard of a dock brief before, but did not know what it meant, but, as soon as she saw that she could have a complete barrister in a wig and gown for £2 4s 6d, she decided that this was the solution, and it made her much happier. She was consequently able to listen to the case of the gentleman in the blue suit with more interest. After he had been duly tried and convicted, it transpired that he had two previous convictions for robbery, and one for attempted murder, and, before he was sentenced, he asked for five other cases to be taken into consideration. The general opinion of the gallery was that he would be imprisoned for ten years, which showed the value of experience, for the judge thought likewise. It would indeed have been quite an interesting day for Lucy but for the reason which had prompted her to go there.

While the nice young man in the blue suit was on his way to Wormwood Scrubs to start his sentence, Lucy was walking home in a rather happier frame of mind. After all, although she'd been stupid and told lies, you can't be sent to prison just for that. There'd be more people in prison than outside it, she said to herself, if that were a crime. And with a barrister all to myself to defend me, I'm bound to get off. So she comforted herself. No doubt she was right in thinking that lies and stupidity by themselves do not qualify a person for prison. But her confidence in a bewigged barrister, price £2 4s 6d, was not altogether justified. As the years go on, more and more is done to assist impecunious litigants, and, from the speeches made in Parliament by the large number of members of the Bar who, for one reason or another, take to a political career, it would seem that everything necessary is done to ensure that a man charged with a crime shall have adequate representation on his trial, however poor he may be. Unfortunately, however, this is far removed from the truth. Representation he can have – often for nothing and always for £2 4s 6d – but adequate representation is another matter. When it is known that a prisoner is about to exercise his right of choosing counsel, numbers of barristers with sufficient practice of their own, walk out of Court so as not to be chosen. At one time there was a practice adopted by some counsel of removing their wigs, but this was abolished as undignified. So now they walk out – leaving behind them the following classes of counsel: (1) those who are already engaged on a case and can successfully plead this as an excuse for not accepting a dock brief; (2) those who are young and inexperienced and want a prisoner to practise on; (3) those who have failed at the Bar and whose only work consists in dock briefs and 'soup.' 'Soup' is the expression used for easy briefs for the prosecution, which are ladled out in rotation to members of a Bar mess.

Three weeks later Lucy surrendered to her bail at the Old Bailey. Although she had managed to keep fairly cheerful up to the moment of surrender, she could truthfully have said 'I don't feel very well' as she stepped into the dock. It must be a very unpleasant experience for those who have not been through it before (and, indeed, for some of those who have) to be called upon to surrender. There you are sitting free in the Court, an ordinary person able to come and go as you please. Suddenly a voice (that of the Clerk of the Court) says loudly, 'John Jones, surrender.' Up you get (begging your pardon) and climb into the dock, where you will either be called upon to stand your trial immediately or from where you will be removed to the cells below until a Court is ready for your trial. Lucy had previously found courage to tell the Clerk of the Court that she wished to employ counsel and that she had £2 4s 6d with which to do it, and accordingly, as soon as she had surrendered to her bail she was called upon to look at the counsel in Court and choose one. There were six on the rank. She asked for a somewhat elderly gentleman whom she rightly thought must have had years of experience of the law. So he had, having spent the last thirty years at the Old Bailey and London Sessions hoping to get dock briefs and 'soup' or anything else that might come his way. Mr Frith Wyndham at once rose and himself entered the dock, following Lucy down the stairs towards one of the consultation rooms where counsel can interview clients in custody.

'Well, what's all this about?' said Mr Wyndham, as soon as they were alone. Lucy told him.

'Dear, dear, dear,' he said, and brought out from his pockets six pencils of different colours.

'Now, I must have the details.'

Lucy did her best to supply them and he wrote them down, using first one pencil and then another, until there was quite an attractive splash of colour on his notebook.

'Now,' said Mr Wyndham, 'perhaps you could tell me how you managed to choose all those winners. Not for my own personal use, you know,' he added with a smile. 'But it's got quite a lot to do with the case.'

'I'd rather not say,' said Lucy.

'Rather not say, eh?' said Mr. Wyndham. 'Oh, well, never mind, I think I understand. We'll do our best, anyway. How old are you?'

'Twenty-two.'

'Any parents?'

Lucy hesitated, then, 'None living,' she said.

'No trouble before?'

'None.'

'All right,' said Mr Wyndham, 'that's all I shall want. Thank you. Good luck to you.' And he went back to the Court.

Not long afterwards, Lucy's case came on and up the stairs she went and stood in the dock with a wardress in attendance. In due course she was called upon to plead to the charges against her. A trial cannot go on until the prisoner pleads 'Guilty' or 'Not Guilty,' but it is no good just refusing to plead in the hope that this will prevent your being tried. In the old days, if you took this course, they would take you to a convenient place, stretch you out on the ground, put weights on your stomach and keep you there in that position, giving you a little bread and water from time to time until you either died or indicated that you would make a plea. For some time past that treatment has been considered too rough. All that would happen nowadays is that a jury would be empanelled and called upon to decide whether you were dumb by the visitation of God or mute of malice. If the jury found you mute of malice, a plea of 'Not Guilty' would be entered and the trial would proceed. If they found you dumb by the visitation of God, you would go to Broadmoor. In Lucy's case this procedure was quite unnecessary and she pleaded 'Not Guilty' to all the charges in a clear but quiet tone. That, by the way, is the best way to plead. Guilty people often yell out 'Not Guilty,' innocent ones never do. In exactly the same way, when a person goes into the witness box and takes the oath, it is only the witness who is about to lie like a trooper who considers it necessary to say the words of the oath at the top of his (or her) voice.

CHAPTER FOUR

Legal Aid

So Lucy's trial began and the evidence given against her was substantially the same as that given at the police Court, but on this occasion she had the opportunity (if not the advantage) of cross-examination on her behalf by Mr Frith Wyndham. Cross-examination is an art. It is often easier than examination of one's own witness (particularly if important issues depend on the evidence of that witness and the witness is either stupid or difficult), though it is usually assumed to be harder. In cross-examination it is as important to know what not to ask as to know what to ask, and all the great cross-examiners have been models in this respect. Mr Frith Wyndham, unfortunately for Lucy, had his own peculiar style. He seldom asked a relevant question, many of his questions developed (as long as the judge would permit it) into little speeches, and it was tolerably certain that the one question which it was essential that he should ask would remain unput. His cross-examination of a witness from Vulgan's went like this.

MR FRITH WYNDHAM: Yours is a very large concern, is it not?

THE WITNESS: Yes.

MR FRITH WYNDHAM: You take bets from all classes of the community?

THE WITNESS: Yes.

MR FRITH WYNDHAM: To the tune of hundreds of thousands of pounds?

THE WITNESS: In a year, very likely.

MR FRITH WYNDHAM (*with a look at the jury*): And most of them lose?

THE WITNESS: Many of them, but not Mr Thompson of 11 Pocket Lane.

MR FRITH WYNDHAM (*loudly*): I was not asking you about Mr Thompson. Will you kindly answer the questions I ask and not those that I do not ask. This is a persecution, not a prosecution.

THE JUDGE: You are not entitled to say that, Mr Wyndham.

MR FRITH WYNDHAM: Am I not to be allowed to conduct my cross-examination in my own way?

THE JUDGE: As long as it is a proper way. Ask questions; don't make speeches.

MR FRITH WYNDHAM: Very well, then, my Lord. Are you not prosecuting this girl?

THE JUDGE: The prosecution is by the King; this witness's employers are only the informants.

MR FRITH WYNDHAM: Are you not the informants, then?

THE JUDGE: I have just said they are.

MR FRITH WYNDHAM: I can't ask your Lordship questions.

THE JUDGE: No.

MR FRITH WYNDHAM: I can only cross-examine the witness.

THE JUDGE: Then pray do so.

MR FRITH WYNDHAM: I was until your Lordship interrupted.

THE JUDGE: There is no need to be impertinent, Mr Wyndham.

MR FRITH WYNDHAM (*to the witness*): Tell me, do you care in your business how many people you ruin?

THE JUDGE: What has this to do with the case?

MR FRITH WYNDHAM: Everything. I say they are trying to ruin this girl.

THE JUDGE: If you wish to put to the witness that information was laid against your client because of malice and not because of the truth of the information, you can do so, but that is a very different question from the one you put.

MR FRITH WYNDHAM: I was leading up to it in my own way.

THE JUDGE (*to the witness*): Do you bear malice towards the accused?

THE WITNESS: No, my Lord.

THE JUDGE: As far as you know, do your employers?

THE WITNESS: No, my Lord.

THE JUDGE: Yes, Mr Frith Wyndham?

MR FRITH WYNDHAM: I wish your Lordship would let me ask the questions.

THE JUDGE: Continue with your cross-examination.

MR FRITH WYNDHAM (*to the witness*): Now, sir, answer this question, Yes or No. Yes or No, d'you understand? (*Witness waits for the question.*) Come now, sir, will you do me the courtesy of answering my question?

THE WITNESS: What question?

MR FRITH WYNDHAM: What question? Will you kindly listen to me, sir?

THE JUDGE: I certainly don't know to what question you are referring, Mr Wyndham.

MR FRITH WYNDHAM: The question was whether he understands that I want an answer, Yes or No, to the next question. He knew well enough what I was asking. Answer me now, sir, Yes or No. D'you hear me, sir, Yes or No. (*Mr Frith Wyndham was shouting by this time.*)

THE JUDGE: There's no need to yell at the witness.

MR FRITH WYNDHAM: From his behaviour he seems to be deaf.

THE JUDGE: He doesn't appear in the least deaf. Are you deaf?

THE WITNESS: No, my Lord.

MR FRITH WYNDHAM: Very well, sir, as you are not deaf (*and Mr Frith Wyndham drops his voice to a melodramatic whisper*) will you kindly answer the question Yes or No.

THE WITNESS: What question?

MR FRITH WYNDHAM: This is intolerable. I appeal to your Lordship for protection.

THE JUDGE: Well, what was the question, Mr Wyndham?

MR FRITH WYNDHAM (*who suddenly has a complete blank in his mind – all barristers and public speakers have had the experience – in an exasperated voice*): Now I've forgotten it.

THE JUDGE (*soothingly*): Well, ask the next question, Mr Wyndham.

MR FRITH WYNDHAM (*flinging his papers on the desk*): I've forgotten that too – (*after a pause*) – I think I will ask your Lordship's permission to retire from this case. I don't feel I can do justice to it. Your Lordship has hardly allowed me to ask a single question without intervening. (*Under his breath but so that the judge can hear*): It's really too bad; never seen anything like it.

THE JUDGE: There's no need to be rude, Mr Wyndham, but you may certainly retire from the case. The defendant may choose another counsel from one of those present.

Lucy, who had been following the proceedings with some dismay, would have liked to have asked for the judge's advice to assist her in making a choice. She felt frightened to do this, however, and she eventually decided on a young man with a very new white wig. This was her first piece of luck. It was true that the young man was very young, but he was a very bright young man indeed, and his lack of experience and knowledge were fully compensated for by his great intelligence and flexibility of mind. Too often in criminal courts head knocks against head and no one has the ability to avoid the useless conflict. There was no chance of this happening with Mr Douglas Croft, who was destined later to become one of the leading advocates of his day.

CHAPTER FIVE

Not Guilty

The trial was adjourned until the next day, and Lucy had an interview with Mr Croft, which differed very much from the one with Mr Frith Wyndham. Within ten minutes Mr Croft had got down to the root of the matter and was pressing Lucy on the one vital point – how had she chosen the winners.

'Now, look here, Miss Smith,' he said, 'you've got to tell me, unless, of course, the whole thing's a fraud. If that's the case, you'd better say so at once. You'll do much better by making a clean breast of it. First offence, your age and all that, you might get away with being bound over.'

'But I'm not guilty,' said Lucy. 'I put those bets on before the races.'

'So you say,' said Mr Croft, 'and it doesn't matter whether I believe you or not, but nobody's going to believe you (and that includes the jury) unless you say how you were able to do it. If you're guilty and won't take my advice about admitting it, well and good, stick to your story; I'll do the best I can, but you'll probably be convicted and very likely go to prison. If you're not guilty, however, you've simply got to tell me all about it. There's absolutely no alternative.'

Lucy hesitated. Then, 'I don't like bringing other people into it,' she said. 'That's why I don't want to tell you.'

'If you prefer to go to prison, that's your affair, but I can assure you that, unless you bring these other people into it, you have a very good chance of spending some time in Holloway. Not a nice place at all. Only been there once. Quite enough. Can't recommend it.'

'All right,' said Lucy. 'I'll tell you. I got the horses from my father.'

'That's better. Who is he – a tipster or a trainer or something?'

'He's the vicar of a small country parish called Tapworth Magna.'

'How on earth could he have given you the winners? I have met a few parsons at race meetings, but really, Miss Smith – '

'It's quite true, but father doesn't go to race meetings. He studies breeding and form, and by a combination of the two he can give you winner after winner. He never backs them himself though.'

'This is extraordinary.'

'I know. It is. That's why I didn't want to tell you about it. He's made a study of it for years. He works out winners, like some people do crosswords. It's quite amazing. I'd never thought anything about it until I went to Vulgan's. I'd often seen him working at it and browsing over his books on breeding, but I'd never even thought of putting on a bet. As I learned more about betting, however, and I found that I was in a perfect position to place bets, not like most people who bet, without half the information that's required, but with everything one needs including the very latest prices, I thought I'd try it and see how good my father really was. Of course, it was against the rules of the firm, but that isn't very terrible. Well, I started. I used to get the information each weekend when I went to stay with my parents. I never told my father. I just pretended to be taking more interest in his hobby.'

'Well, it's a strange story, but, if it's true, we'll have to call your father as a witness.'

'That's what I was afraid of.'

'I can't help it. It's quite essential. You must get him up to town at once.'

After a certain amount of further argument, Lucy was finally persuaded to tell the whole story to her parents, with the result that the trial was adjourned until the next session, and, when her new trial began before a different judge and jury, her father was the second witness for the defence. Mr Croft had rightly assumed that the judge would decide to test Mr Meeson-Smith's powers and he had warned him to work out some winners. So it came about that the questions with which this tale began were asked and answered.

When the trial was resumed, it was known that all four horses had won. In consequence the Court was crowded and the press took a very great interest in the case, most of their representatives being anxious to interview the vicar at the first opportunity, and to make him tempting offers to sell his methods of picking winners for the benefit of their public. The judge, Mr Justice Painswick, who himself took no interest whatever in betting or horse racing, was surprised at the excitement which the trial was causing. 'Money for nothing, I suppose,' he said to himself.

Immediately on the resumption of the trial the vicar went back into the witness box.

'Well, Mr Meeson-Smith,' said the judge, 'you seem to have been singularly successful in your forecasts.'

'Not singularly, I hope, my Lord. I do, of course, from time to time have failures, due in most cases to causes beyond my control, as, for instance, when a horse is not as fit as his trainer thinks or the like, but normally I can find the winner in such races. If your Lordship would care for me to explain how I do it – '

Those in Court waited expectantly.

'I think not at the moment, thank you,' said the judge. 'The point is that you have sworn you gave to the accused the various winners which the accused backed and unquestionably you have now provided some concrete evidence of your ability to choose winners. What do you say, Mr Trumper, do you agree that the evidence is sufficient on this matter or would you like a further test, if Mr Croft has no objection?'

Now Mr Trumper, unlike the judge, was a regular attendant at racecourses and he had been kicking himself for not having backed a single one of the vicar's selections. He did not back the first of them for two reasons. In the first place he did not for a moment believe in the vicar's powers and still thought that the whole thing was a fraud; secondly, the vicar's first horse did not coincide with the strong stable tip he had received from a friend. When the vicar's horse won he considered it a fluke, and so he did not back the second. He did not back the third as he felt certain that the vicar's luck would not hold, while, although he intended to back the fourth, there was a slight misunderstanding between him and his wife as to which of them should put the money on and each thought the other had done it. The odds were highly remunerative for the backer, and when Mr Trumper returned home with the news that it had won at 100 to 8, Mr and Mrs Trumper, who thought they had invested a flyer on it, opened a bottle of champagne. It was only while they were drinking the second glass that they discovered that neither of them had backed it. It was then too late to replace the cork. He was not quite certain how to answer the judge's question. To do him justice, he only had in mind the interests of the prosecution. No doubt if the case were adjourned for a further test, he would have another chance of making use of the vicar's skill; equally, no doubt, however, in that event most members of the public would put their money on and the odds would be hopeless from the backer's point of view; on the other hand, if there were no adjournment, he might be able to persuade his learned friend Mr Croft to obtain the information from the witness and give it to him privately. Mr Trumper paid no regard to such considerations. He thought for a few moments, and then: 'My Lord,' he said, 'in view of the fact that I did not originally suggest that the test proposed was not sufficient, I do not think I ought to keep this prosecution hanging over the head of the accused longer than is necessary, by asking for a further adjournment. I think that the prosecution must accept that the witness has reasonably established his ability to have done what he says he did. Whether he did it or not will, of course, be a question for the jury.'

It is to be observed that it is no part of the duty of the prosecution in England to seek to secure the conviction of the accused, but only to see that all the facts are fairly brought before the Court. Mr Trumper was living up to this high tradition, which is nearly always observed by counsel for the Crown in cases which are obviously crumbling and in which there is no reasonable chance of obtaining a conviction.

'Well, Mr Trumper,' went on the judge, 'if you accept the evidence that Mr Meeson-Smith could have given his daughter the names of the horses involved, do you think you should proceed further with the case? Both he and the accused have sworn that he did so, and there is no evidence whatever that the bets were placed after the results of the races were known. You originally asked the jury to draw the inference that they were so placed by reason of two factors: first, the inherent improbability of anyone being able to find so many winners; secondly, the false statements made by the accused when challenged. Both these matters have been explained, the former by the present witness and the latter by reason of the rule that employees may not bet with the firm. Quite rightly, in my view, the prosecution has based its case on real dishonesty, not a breach of the regulations. It might have been possible to charge the accused with an offence by reason of false representations that a Mr Thompson was making the bets when she knew that they would not have been accepted if she made them in her own name. That, however, is no part of your case, and I think you made it plain to the jury that the whole essence of the case for the prosecution was that the bets were placed after the races.'

'That is quite true, my Lord. Will your Lordship forgive me for a minute?'

'Certainly.'

Mr Trumper conferred with the solicitor instructing him for a few moments, and then, following the tradition to which reference has been made, he said: 'My Lord, the prosecution does not desire to ask the jury to convict the accused on this evidence.'

'A very proper course, Mr Trumper.'

A few seconds later the jury returned a verdict of 'Not Guilty,' and Lucy was discharged.

CHAPTER SIX

On Obtaining Credit

As soon as he was in the corridor the vicar was surrounded by representatives of the press. Normally, an attractive young woman, who had been acquitted, would have been the object of their attention, but on this occasion they were mainly interested in her father.

'Please, please, gentlemen,' protested the vicar. 'I think it most kind of you to give me your good wishes. I am, of course, delighted that my daughter's name has been cleared, but I have no other statement to make.'

'What about a tip for tomorrow?'

'Please, gentlemen, you must understand. I am not a tipster, nor do I back horses. I get great entertainment from the study of the breeding and form of racehorses, but I am not interested in making money out of it. It is true that I do in fact work out what I might have won by accumulators and mixed doubles and trebles and so forth. But I only do that as an arithmetical exercise.' At last he managed to escape with Lucy, but not for very long. They had not been in the room at his hotel for more than ten minutes before a representative of the *Daily Sun* managed to break in on them.

'Forgive me,' he said. 'I had to see you.'

'About what, pray?'

'I'll tell you. I know you don't want any money for yourself, but I am sure you could do with some for your church or for the poorer people in your parish. How about a new organ, for instance?'

'It's very kind of you, but we do not require a new organ.'

'Well, another village hall or a fund for the old people. Now, look here, you can name your own price within reason. If you'll let me have two horses a week with or without an article on how you select them, I'll give you whatever you want. That's fair, isn't it?'

'Very kind, indeed, but I'm afraid it's no good, sir. I should not feel comfortable about it. I enjoy my little hobby and, if people choose to bet within their means I am sufficiently broad-minded, I hope, not to consider them beyond the pale. But I cannot do anything to encourage gambling or to lead people to believe that there is any other proper way of obtaining wealth except by hard work.'

'Hard work won't produce wealth these days if it's honest.'

'My dear sir, I'm afraid I cannot argue with you on the merits or consequences of income tax and surtax. The means of livelihood, great or small, should be obtained by work and not by the toss of a coin or the nose of a horse. I'm very sorry, but I cannot assist you.'

After a few further attempts the newspaper man had to admit defeat and Lucy and her father were left alone for about ten more minutes, when they were again interrupted. The lounge of their hotel was full of people of all kinds anxious to make contact with one whom they termed a certain money spinner.

While they were engaged in dealing with the consequent interruptions, Mr Justice Painswick was on his way home from the Old Bailey. He lived in a small flat in South Kensington and often, when the weather was fine, and he had no engagement, he walked home. He was a widower with one grown-up son and his interests outside the law and his son were mainly in literature, ancient and modern, and monumental brasses. As he walked he was deep in thought. He was not thinking, as some judges might have been, how iniquitous it was that by the use of the methods adopted by Mr Meeson-Smith a man might make thousands of pounds a year free of tax without rendering any service to the State, whilst a High Court Judge had an annual income of £5,000, about half of which was taken away in taxation. He was trying to see the point of a joke he had read in a newspaper and, at the same time, to translate it into Latin elegiacs. He had not succeeded in either task by the time he arrived home, but it made the journey seem extremely short.

There was a visitor waiting for him. He did not know the man and said a trifle impatiently: 'What can I do for you, sir?'

'I'm very sorry to trouble you, Sir Charles, but it's a matter of some importance.'

'I'm afraid I don't even know who you are.'

'Quite. It's about your son.'

Mr Justice Painswick was unfortunate in his son. He was always getting into trouble of one kind or another and the judge had more than once been called upon to find substantial sums of money to prevent him from being made bankrupt. In spite of everything, the judge remained devoted to him and ready to do anything in his power to help him. He wondered what it was this time.

'Very well, then, Mr – Mr – '

'Fuller.'

'Please come in and sit down.' They went into the sitting-room.

'Nasty business, I'm afraid,' began Mr Fuller.

'In what way?'

'You've just come from the Old Bailey, I believe?'

'What has that to do with it?'

'That's where I may be quite soon.'

'How does that concern my son?'

'He'll come with me.'

'Please explain yourself.'

'Of course. That's what I'm here for.'

As Mr Fuller plunged into the details, Mr Justice Painswick became more and more worried. The man might be lying, but there was the stamp of truth on most of what he said. In short, it came to this, that Fuller and his son were in partnership, that they had been buying goods on credit and selling them below cost for cash and that this had been done on such a scale that, unless the pressing creditors were satisfied, there was every likelihood of a prosecution for fraud.

'You've come for money, of course,' said the judge.

'Naturally, but equally I don't expect you to part with a penny until I've satisfied you of the truth of what I've said.'

'How much is needed?'

'Rather a lot, I'm afraid. The total debts are about £30,000, but if we could have £20,000 we could probably get out all right.'

'£20,000,' said the judge. 'It's quite impossible.'

It was, indeed. Most of his savings had already gone, first in setting up his son in a profession and later in paying his debts. His profession was that of an accountant, while his business ventures varied. The fact that he was an accountant, the judge appreciated, would make his defence to a prosecution for fraud even more difficult.

'Well, there it is,' said Fuller. '£20,000 or it's the high jump for us. I don't expect you to mind about me, but I thought you might want to help Martin.'

The judge did want to help him. He had a vivid imagination and he could already visualise Court proceedings, the paragraphs in the paper, the trial at the Old Bailey, and (probably) Wormwood Scrubs after the trial. It would be very awkward for him as a judge, but that was his least worry. He did not want his son to go to prison. There was no impropriety in paying his debts, and, if he had had the money, he would not have hesitated. However, he simply had not got it, or anything like it.

'Where is Martin now?' he said. 'He'd better come to see me.'

'He's in Norfolk, but he'll come and see you as soon as I tell him you'll help.'

'I said nothing about help. I wish to see him.' The judge was beginning to have a very faint hope that Fuller was lying to him.

'Oh, very well, I'll send him along, and I'll tell him to bring the evidence too.'

The interview ended shortly afterwards and the judge spent a very troubled night. A few days later Martin called on him and they went into the matter together.

Martin was a very pleasant young man to meet, provided he had not selected you as his victim; there is, however, no doubt at all but that he had inherited the criminal instincts of one of his ancestors, who had been a highwayman. It is strange how very respectable and conscientious parents can produce a reprobate, but so it is throughout the animal world. As the Reverend Wellsby Meeson-Smith had discovered in the case of horses, the qualities of a father may apparently miss the son and be strongly developed in the grandson. In the case of Martin Painswick one had to go much further back than the grandfather, but unquestionably Uriah Painswick, who eventually established (by means of his ill-gotten gains) a large and profitable hostelry on the Portsmouth Road, had had a most determined and unusually successful criminal career, until he had made enough to enable him to retire. Had he been caught and executed, as he certainly deserved to have been, there would have been no Mr Justice Painswick and his famous judgments (which made sense of most of the Rent Restriction Acts without repealing or altering very much of them) would never have been delivered.

Martin was very cheerful as he talked to his father.

'It's so easy,' he was saying. 'You don't even need to write yourself any references. Anyone can get credit if he pays enough in cash to begin with. We only had £500, and, d'you know, we owe about £30,000. Pretty good, isn't it?'

'You're just a hooligan, Martin,' said his father, 'but, apart from the criminality of it, how d'you expect to make it pay? If you sell below cost, you're bound to make a loss.'

'Ah, but we have the use of the cash, you see. We might back a horse or do a flutter on the Stock Exchange, and so on, etcetera, and make a packet. We could never borrow the money from anyone, you see, unless, of course, we did a bit of kite flying and that's such a nerve-racking job. So we just go into any old business (we're in ladies' underwear at the moment – with a few sidelines in lampshades, ironmongery, and so on, etcetera) establish our credit by paying cash, and, hey presto, we've as much as we want to take us to Goodwood. See the idea?'

'I *know* the idea. I've sent plenty of people to jail for using it.'

'Hope I don't come up in front of you. That'd be awkward.'

The judge sighed. Time and again he had asked himself why he had such an affection for this criminal he had brought into the world. Time and again he had tried to bring himself to send Martin out of his life. But resolute as he was in the normal way, he was hopelessly irresolute in the case of his son. Martin was all he had left of his marriage and he could not give him up.

'Well, I don't know what I can do for you,' he said. 'Even if I were prepared to assist, I couldn't find anything like the sum you need.'

'Oh, well, it can't be helped,' said his son. 'Very decent of you even to think of it after last time. That cost you a pretty penny, I'm afraid. Oh, well,' he added, 'perhaps we'll have to do a little kite flying after all. That will tide it over, but it's such a strenuous game. I hate it.'

'Kite flying' is a method of borrowing money from a bank, which is not prepared to lend it to you. Here is the recipe, but you should understand that it normally constitutes the crime of obtaining money by false pretences and you are not recommended to try it.

1. Take two or three banks. Call them Banks A, B and C.
2. Open accounts in different names at each of them or preferably get friends or acquaintances of yours to do so.
3. Obtain cheque books from each of the banks.
4. Select the bank with the most promising manager. The ordinary respectable member of the public who is accustomed to receive a warning letter from his bank manager, when his account is £1 2s 4d overdrawn, will be surprised to learn that

you can get almost anything out of some bank managers, providing you are flying high enough. A High Court judge, who has no security to offer, may not be able to obtain a £500 overdraft from a bank, but a foreign trickster with the gift of the gab can cheat a bank out of thousands of pounds. Impossible, you say. Well, it happens. Sometimes the trickster goes to prison for quite a long time, but, provided he is lucky in his gambling or business ventures and repays the money in time, nothing happens to him at all except that the head-waiters at the big hotels are particularly polite to him.

5. Assume that you have selected Bank A as having the bank manager best fulfilling your requirements. Draw, or as the case may be get your friend to draw, a cheque in your favour for, say, £50 on Bank B. Pay this cheque into Bank A and ask that bank to let you have, say, £40 against the uncleared cheque. Once you have the £40 you can do what you like with it, but somehow or other you have got to pay £50 into Bank B in order to meet the cheque. Assume you put the £40 on a horse and it loses, you must at once draw a cheque for £100 on Bank C, pay it into Bank A and ask for, say, £80 against it. Having got the £80, rush round to Bank B and pay in £50 to meet the first cheque. You now have £30 to put on a horse, but you have got to meet the £100 cheque drawn on Bank C. If the next horse loses, draw a cheque on Bank B for £200 and pay it into Bank A (which has by this time cleared the £50 cheque) and ask for, say, £150 against it. Take £100 of this to Bank C to meet the £100 cheque and put the remaining £50

on a horse. If, by chance, it wins at sufficiently good odds, you can meet the cheque for £200 out of your winnings, and all is well. You have been able in effect to borrow money from Bank A to finance your betting transactions. Assuming, however, that the third horse loses you must continue with the previous procedure, the amount of the cheques going up and up. All will go well unless and until Bank A refuses to give you cash against uncleared cheques. Then the balloon will go up and you with it, unless, of course, you are like Martin Painswick and have a father, who is really fond of you and prepared to pay your debts, or unless you have other facilities for reimbursing the bank.

There is no copyright in this recipe, which has been used hundreds and hundreds of times with success, and is still being used. Only the other day a bank lost some £50,000 or £60,000 in this way. It is true that the gentleman concerned (whose horses or business ventures, and so on, etcetera, always seemed to fail) went to prison for quite a long time, but, had they been successful, he would have become a big businessman who owed his success to borrowing huge sums of money from a bank on no security free of interest.

As Martin Painswick remarked, however, it is a nerve racking business. You always have a cheque to meet and no money to meet it with, unless the bank is prepared to go on advancing money against your worthless cheque. Every day there is the chance that the snowball will melt.

'I shouldn't do that,' said Mr Justice Painswick. 'I might manage to let you have £5,000, but that's absolutely the limit.'

'That is decent of you, father, but I'm afraid it's nothing like enough. Our creditors are so vindictive. I really don't see why they should be. They only gave us credit to make profits themselves. If they chose to take the risk, that's their fault.'

'They thought they were dealing with honest traders. If they had been, they would have been most unlikely to lose so much.'

'Oh well, there it is. You'll come and see me in prison sometimes, won't you?'

'You're incorrigible. How quickly must you find the money?'

'At once, really. We might hang on for a month or so, but not more. We shouldn't have troubled you if we could have managed without.'

'Well, go away now. I'll see if there's anything I can do, but I don't see what there is. Leave me your address.'

Ten minutes later Martin was gone and his father was racking his brains to see if there was anyone from whom he could borrow the money. But it was quite hopeless. There were few people he could ask for a loan for such a purpose and none of them could have made it. It seemed that the end had really come and that Martin would be sent to prison. Then he picked up the evening paper and, looking at the cricket scores, he happened to notice the headline: 'HALFPENNY IS THE RIGHT SORT FOR ASCOT.' Suddenly, for the first time since he had left the Old Bailey some few days before, he thought of the Reverend Wellsby Meeson-Smith and his apparent ability to find winners. He thought for a few minutes. There is nothing wrong in backing horses. Royalty goes to the Derby and Ascot. A High Court judge shouldn't bet regularly, but no one would complain of an odd wager or two. Suppose he staked £1,000; if he had the help of the Reverend Wellsby

Meeson-Smith he might turn it quickly into £20,000. If he lost it all, the loss wouldn't break him. There was no other means of obtaining the money. The judge was a man of quick decision. He seldom reserved judgment. After a little further thought he decided to visit Tapworth Magna, to place his problem before the vicar, and try to enlist his help. It would be extremely embarrassing to him, but there was no other way, and at any rate there could be no harm in going to see the vicar. Once he had made his decision, he acted quickly. He telephoned to the local inn at Tapworth Magna and asked for a room. After some consultation between the landlord and his wife, he was told he could have a bed in the billiard room if he could put up with that. The fact was that Tapworth Magna had suddenly become the centre of interest of a large percentage of the British population. It was a small, fairly isolated parish of about some 400 souls, with an old church, a general store and post office combined, a butcher, and an inn which could accommodate a very few visitors. The nearest town was about five miles away. Every hotel there was crowded out. There was, in effect, a pilgrimage, the goal of which was the vicarage at Tapworth Magna, or rather the store of knowledge in the mind of its vicar. The landlord of The Fox at Tapworth Magna did not mention that the judge would be sharing the billiard room with three other people, but he had consulted with his wife as to whether they could squeeze in another. The judge accepted, and a few hours later was on his way.

CHAPTER SEVEN

A Room for the Night

The journey to Tapworth Magna is a simple one. You take the train to Poppleton and enjoy a pleasant drive by taxi from Poppleton station. The whole journey takes about two and a half hours from London, and, shortly before closing time on a Saturday evening in June, Mr Justice Painswick arrived at The Fox. He was surprised to find the inn crowded. His reception by the landlord was polite but rather more offhand than he could have wished. He had given his name as Sir Charles Painswick. Perhaps they did not know his position. Even if they had done so, however, on this occasion it would have made little difference. The landlord of The Fox was at the moment a very important person indeed. He was a most useful link between his guests and the vicar, and he had promised most of them an introduction. Like the various elixirs sought after in the seventeenth century, the vicar's ability to name (in advance) the winners of horse races was becoming more and more the object of the search of a vast quantity of human beings who were otherwise normal. How could a mere High Court judge compete? Apart altogether from the special circumstances obtaining at Tapworth Magna, it may not be out of place to consider his position in and out of Court.

Sitting in his Court he appears to be a person of supreme importance. Treated by many with awe and by everyone with respect, he is master in his own Court and what he says is law, at any rate until he is reversed in the Court of Appeal.

'Silence in Court,' says the usher as the judge comes in. Everyone rises and is silent. Anyone who deliberately and persistently ignored the usher's warning would be fined or sent to prison for contempt of Court, or both. Counsel bow to the judge, some obsequiously and some more naturally, but they all bow. The judge returns their salute and sits down. He beams or scowls around him as he pleases. Counsel rises to make an application. He wishes to mention the last case in the list which has been compromised and to go quickly to another Court where he holds an important brief.

'Might I mention to your Lordship – ' he begins.

'No,' says the judge, 'not for the moment.'

It is inconvenient for counsel, highly inconvenient, but there is nothing he can do about it. The judge taps with his pencil to indicate that he wishes to speak to the associate, the Court official who sits below him. The associate stands up on his chair to speak to the judge. There is a whispered conversation between them. After a short time the judge says: 'Who is in the last case?'

Counsel leaps to his feet. 'I am, my Lord. My learned friend Mr Noble is against me. I wanted to mention to your Lordship – '

'Wait a moment, then. How long is the case likely to take, Mr Noble?'

Before Mr Noble can rise, counsel on his feet says: 'Less than a minute, my Lord. It is settled.'

'Oh,' says the judge. 'I asked, Mr Noble. Is that right, Mr Noble?'

'Yes, my Lord.'

'Oh, very well – is there anything which requires my consent? Are the parties *sui juris*?'

'Yes, my Lord.'

'Very well then, endorse your briefs with the terms agreed and hand them in to the associate.'

Both counsel bow and the judge gives a slight smile in the direction of Mr Noble and ignores the other. Then they retire. The first case is called on. Counsel opens the case and witnesses go into the box and are examined and cross-examined.

'Stand up, sir, and take your hands out of your pockets,' says the judge to one witness, who gave a somewhat pert answer to which the judge could think of no other rejoinder.

'Pay proper respect to the Court.'

'I'm very sorry, my Lord,' says the witness and, indeed, looks it.

And so the case goes on. Right or wrong, the judge holds his sway. Woe betide the litigant who tries to cross him. Woe betide most counsel – not quite all – who try conclusions with him.

'But, my Lord, I respectfully submit that the evidence is not to be looked at in that way.'

'That is how I look at it.'

'I hope your Lordship will hear me on the subject.'

'I can't help hearing you,' says the judge. A titter goes round the Court. The judge has scored off counsel. How very easy it is for the man on top to make the man down below look small. If the judge makes a joke, everyone laughs. That is not good for the judge's standard of humour. If everyone always laughs, he can never tell whether the joke was really worth laughing at. The case goes on and on, witnesses come and go and counsel continue with their respectful submissions. Eventually, at 4.15 p.m., the judge rises, goes to his room, takes off his robes and leaves the Law Courts.

How are the mighty fallen. That same judge, whose word up to a few minutes ago was at least temporary law, wants a packet of cigarettes.

'Sorry, no cigarettes,' says the pert young lady behind the counter.

'But I thought – ' begins the judge.

'Can't you read?' says the young lady. This is surely the most terrible contempt of Court. But no it isn't; the judge is out of his Court and in the young lady's. He gets in an omnibus, and has to stand.

'Come along there, move up to the end,' says the conductor.

'I'm getting out in a moment,' says the judge.

'I can't help that, move up to the end, please,' and the judge has to move.

He goes to the box-office of a theatre where a popular play is being performed. He wants a seat for that evening.

'Have you – ' he begins.

'Nothing at all,' snaps the box-office manager, in the odious tone employed by most box-office managers as long as the play is a success.

He goes to a cinema. He has to stand in a queue. Again, as in the omnibus, he is ordered about like a schoolboy and has to obey or go.

Eventually he enters the cinema. He wants to go to the seats on the right. He is directed by a smart usherette to those on the left. He tries to argue, but it is of no avail. The usherette treats him quite as sharply as he has ever treated counsel.

Whether the judge likes it or not, that is how it is. In the High Court of Justice, Strand, WC, the judge is a great man, but, when Esmeralda says 'No,' that same judge can do nothing except respectfully submit.

So it was with Mr Justice Painswick at The Fox. The billiard room in which he was to sleep was full of smoke and people when he arrived. It was a small room with a half-size table, and, even in normal times, it had a musty smell. He enquired from someone when it was closing time in that district. He was longing for bed, although he wondered how he should be able to sleep in such an atmosphere. 'Lots of time,' was the reply. 'Old Pollock has gone into Poppleton.' The judge rightly assumed that Pollock was the local police constable. 'Have a beer?' said his informant generously. 'Thank you very much,' said the judge. It seemed the easiest thing to do. With some difficulty two beers were obtained.

'You on the job too, I suppose?' asked the judge's companion. That was a little difficult for the judge to answer. He was very definitely on the job, but it would be awkward to admit it. At the same time, he did not like to deny it.

'Most people here are, I imagine,' he answered.

'I should say so. I'm from the *Sporting King*. Who are you for?'

'Myself,' said the judge.

'Oh, one of those. You won't get anything. He's as close as they make 'em.'

'Have another beer,' said the judge.

'Don't mind if I do.'

During the ensuing minutes the judge managed to turn the conversation from the vicar to the neighbourhood. His companion, who had only been there four days, knew a great deal about it.

'There's Mrs Poulter,' he told the judge. 'She lives next door to the vicar – only half a mile away from the

51

vicarage. She's a charming woman with two children. Unfortunately she lives above her income and, ever since the news leaked out, she's been trying to persuade him to give her some tips. She's even tried to use her children to pump him, but no luck yet. You'll see her in church tomorrow – I suppose you'll go. Everyone will. You'll have to be there early. She wears big hats and has a lovely nose. Then there's Mrs Pace who runs the grocer's and post office. You can't say anything on the telephone without her knowing. She has all the news first. Of course, she's pretty tired at the moment. The telephone's been ringing nearly all the time somewhere in the neighbourhood.' He paused for breath, but soon recovered. 'Oh, I didn't tell you. She's got rather an attractive stammer.'

'How awkward for a telephone operator.'

'Oh, I didn't mean her. I was thinking of Mrs Poulter. As a matter of fact I think of her quite a lot. Yes, she says "W-won't you come in?" Even if she said "G-go away," it would sound attractive, though it wouldn't be as nice. See what I mean?' and he gave the judge a sharp dig in the ribs.

'You old devil, you,' he added.

The judge now appreciated that the two beers they had just consumed were not the first his companion had had. As a matter of fact, he had been drinking solidly for two hours. On the whole, High Court judges do not like being dug in the ribs and called 'you old devil,' but there was nothing that this one could do about it.

'I think I'll be turning in now,' he said as a pretext for moving away.

'Turning in? You won't be able to for a bit. Not with all these people here. You're sleeping here with me, you know.'

'With you?'

This was a most unpleasant shock.

'Oh, yes, and a couple of others. I shouldn't be surprised if there were six of us before we finished. But we'll manage. All good chaps, you know. We have quite a bit of fun.' The judge was beginning to wish he had never started on the adventure. It would probably fail, anyway. He hadn't realised that so many people would be after the same thing.

'Well, I must see about my suitcase.' He eventually managed to get near enough to the landlord to speak to him.

'I understood I was to have the billiard room,' he said.

'That's right, sir. In here. It'll be a bit of a tight squeeze, I'm afraid, but I don't suppose you'll mind. My wife's brother's just come down as well, but we'll fix you up. Anyway, it's all in a good cause. Excuse me, sir,' and the landlord moved off to serve another customer. So it was true. Painswick, J, who had appeared as Judge of Assize at the county town twelve miles away, who had sat in the Court of Appeal, who was spoken of as a likely candidate for the House of Lords, who was one of His Majesty's most dignified judges was about to doss down – there was no other word for it – next to a drunken journalist and three or four others, possibly all drunk. It was horrible. But it was too late to go home now. What could he do? He thought of calling on Mrs Poulter and throwing himself on her mercy. But, then, she apparently had no husband, so that wouldn't do. Then, suddenly, he had a brainwave. He would try the vicar himself. He was not in the habit of using the importance of his position for the purpose of obtaining favours, but he felt desperate now. He must try. The thought of one night in that room with the smell of drink and smoke and the three or four bodies near him filled him almost with terror. He enquired for the vicarage and set out at once, carrying his case. It was a good half-hour's walk and he was not there until past eleven. The house was in darkness. He paused for a moment and then the thought of the billiard room gave him courage and he gave a hard pull at the bell handle. It came off, but otherwise nothing happened. Then he began to knock; first one gentle knock; then two equally gentle; then a third not so gentle, and a fourth, and so on. Probably you have been through the same experience, and the judge was becoming frantic. He had just finished the most thunderous tattoo, putting all his weight behind it, when the door opened and he nearly fell in. It was Lucy.

'What on earth do you want at this time of night?' she said. 'Everyone's in bed. Is someone ill?'

'Not exactly,' said the judge.

'Well, really!' said Lucy. 'What have you come here for?'

The judge could now see who it was as she had a candle with her (there was no gas or electricity at the vicarage). Lucy, on the other hand, did not recognise the judge without his wig and would probably not have done so even in daylight.

There was nothing for it. He was making no progress like this.

'I must apologise very humbly for calling at such an hour, but I am Sir Charles Painswick. You may remember me; I presided at your trial.'

'Good heavens,' said Lucy, 'you can't be. Such things don't happen.'

'They have happened. I have come down to see your father and I had a room at the local inn. The Fox, I think it is called. Unfortunately I am expected to share the billiard room with several other men, one at least of whom is not too sober. I know that I am behaving in a most unusual fashion, and I shall fully understand if you say you cannot help me, but I must admit that I have called to know if of your charity you can give me a bed for the night.'

'Well,' said Lucy, 'who would have thought it? But how do I know you really are Sir Charles?'

'I have my identity card, and, I believe, some letters addressed to me.'

'I must go and speak to mother. D'you mind waiting here for a moment?'

'Of course not.'

In the result, Mr Justice Painswick spent the night at the vicarage, in a large, sparsely-furnished room, with no light except a candle. There was a water jug and basin, but there was no water in the jug. Lucy explained to him that they had no water laid on to the vicarage and that they were dependent on rainwater and a nearby well. Owing to the recent drought the water situation was serious for the Meeson-Smiths. This necessitated a slightly technical explanation to the judge about his use of the sanitary arrangements. Considering their first encounter, as prisoner and judge, Lucy rather enjoyed giving this explanation. But she did not do it out of devilment; it was absolutely necessary.

CHAPTER EIGHT

A Sermon

Next morning the judge was called by Lucy with a cup of tea and about a pint of hot water, which was to do for shaving, washing and cleaning his teeth. But the birds were singing, the view from his window was lovely, Lucy was a pretty girl and he felt extremely cheerful. It was a new adventure and, for all its inconveniences, there was an atmosphere of friendliness about the vicarage which charmed him and made him feel younger. Rabbits were playing undisturbed on the lawn. No doubt they did considerable damage, but no one seemed to mind. The vicar's income was plainly small, the house was in a poor state of repair, but it was obvious that all was well. You can't be more than happy, thought the judge. Meanwhile, the vicar, who was dressing, was in a state of some excitement. He was not at all a worldly man, as was evidenced by his refusal to become wealthy or even to improve, his financial position by backing horses when he could so easily have done so and needed the extra money. On the other hand, he had considerable respect for the great, and he considered that it was an honour to entertain one of His Majesty's judges. As he got dressed he chattered to his wife about it.

'This is most interesting, Caroline,' he said. 'There is so much I should like to ask him.'

'I wonder what he wants to ask you,' said his wife.

'Oh, I expect it's about Lucy, you know. Many judges are very human. I suppose they follow up their cases sometimes. A terrible responsibility it must be, wondering what sentence to impose on some wretched creature and picturing the home of the prisoner, his wife and his children. I should not care for it. Then the dreadful death penalty. To think that the judge, who sentenced Morgan Wilding to death, will be sitting at our breakfast table eating our bacon and eggs.'

'Our eggs,' corrected Caroline.

'What he could tell us, if he chose!'

At that precise moment the judge was thinking what the vicar could tell him if he chose. Shortly afterwards they were all together having breakfast.

'I cannot tell you how grateful I am,' the judge was saying.

'We are only too pleased. We do not often have such an opportunity.'

'How did you think I looked in the dock?' said Lucy.

'Lucy,' said her mother, 'you really mustn't ask such questions.'

'Why not? As father said, one doesn't often get such an opportunity. I don't suppose Sir Charles has ever had breakfast with one of his customers before.'

And so the conversation went on cheerfully, and the judge did not hint at the reason for his visit and the vicar did not dream of asking. The time came for Matins and the vicar was delighted when the judge said he would like to come. Almost immediately he was asked to read the Lessons.

'I'm afraid our congregation is rather small and, unless George Sudbury is there, I should have to read them myself. I expect George will be in bed. His heart's in the right place but I wish he spent half as much time in church as he does in The Fox. Mark you, I've nothing against The Fox, or beer for that matter; I've very little against anything healthy, and beer's healthy enough in the right quantity. Now I'm preaching to you and you'll have enough of that all too soon.'

The judge wondered how the vicar would take the shock of his swollen congregation. He also felt awkward about reading the Lessons. He would enjoy the actual reading; he had a good voice and could give full value to language. But it would bring him very much into prominence and, with all those journalists there, he was very likely to be recognised. However, he did not feel he could refuse.

On the way to church (Caroline and Lucy had gone ahead on bicycles; the judge went with the vicar in the vicar's ancient car, driven slowly and dangerously by him) – the judge mentioned his interest in brasses. The vicar was overjoyed.

'I so seldom find anyone interested,' he said, 'and yet here in Tapworth we have what I believe to be a fragment older than Sir John D'Abernon.'

'Have you, indeed? I confess I had never heard of it. Can you give it a date or a period?'

The judge was frankly sceptical. He had a considerable knowledge of the subject and thought it most odd that neither Macklin nor any other books on the subject, which he had read, referred to it.

'Well,' said the vicar confidentially, 'I am tired of telling them. No one will believe me, but for reasons which, if it will interest you, I will explain in great detail, I would say that it was at least twenty years older than the D'Abernon brass. I would put it at about 1250. Of course, it's only a fragment. When I think of the way those journalists wanted me to talk about my silly horses, it annoys me to feel that they aren't in the least interested in my fragment. Oh, perhaps you don't know about my horses – but then, of course, you do. I told you about them in Court.'

The judge took the opportunity offered.

'I should be most interested to hear about your hobby later,' he said. 'I'm afraid I know nothing of the subject. I've never been to a horse race or backed a horse. But, yes, I did. I once backed the winner of the Derby. Now what was its name? Something about a parade, I think.'

'Ah, that would be Grand Parade in 1919, a poor Derby winner and not a Classic sire.'

'I think I won about seven and six or something?'

'Seven and six? Surely more than that, or else you only put about threepence on it. If my recollection is right it won at 33 to 1.'

'I think it was threepence,' said the judge.

'Dear, dear, well that was a pleasant surprise for you, but I'm glad it didn't start you on the downward path. That's how most people lose their money. A lucky bet to begin with spells ruin. Incredible that so many people think they can make money at it. How do they imagine bookmakers live?'

'Then does no one win except the bookmakers?'

'Practically no one. Of course there are heavy gambles at short odds which do come off, but the people who make them usually lose it all and more in the same way. Oh, no, it's a hopeless game, but colourful of course.'

The judge was a little worried. Did the vicar mean that even he couldn't make money? If so, the prospect of seeing a fragment of a brass believed (by the vicar but by no one else) to be *c*1250 would be a small consolation.

But by this time they had reached the church and further conversation on the subject had to be postponed.

'Good gracious,' said the vicar, 'it looks like a point-to-point.'

The cars were everywhere.

'What on earth has happened? Can they know that you are here, perhaps?' And he turned to the judge.

Never in the history of Tapworth Magna, or any other village for that matter, had such a crowd assembled for morning service on Sunday. In point of numbers it rivalled a fashionable wedding at St Margaret's, Westminster.

'I think perhaps they are interested in you and your hobby, vicar.'

'Dear me. Well, it's an ill wind. I hope I shall rise to the occasion in my sermon. I seldom write them, you know,' he went on, as they made their way with some difficulty to the church door. 'I choose my subject, sometimes a text as well, and then I look at my congregation for inspiration. That means that usually my sermons last about five minutes. I wonder what will happen today?'

Those were the last words they exchanged before the service. They were almost immediately separated by the crowd. The vicar went in to prepare himself and eventually the judge managed to enter the church. It was absolutely packed, and at first sight it seemed that every pew was taken. Then he suddenly discovered two small rows at the back, with room for six people, quite empty. He quickly occupied the gangway seat in the back row. There was a card on the ledge of the front pew with something written on it. From where he sat the lettering was upside down and, though he tried, he was unable to make it out. However, when he came back from reading the first Lesson, he managed to see what it was:

CEILING OVERHEAD IS DANGEROUS

He decided to take the risk and remained in the same place for the rest of the service.

The time came for the sermon and, as the vicar walked up into the pulpit, a sense of expectation held the congregation. Few of them were regular churchgoers, but they wanted to hear what this miracle man had to tell them – even upon a religious subject. The weight of taxation has turned more and more people to gambling in a big or small way. That is the only means, they feel, by which they can honestly acquire riches not subject to tax. Occasionally it dawns on some of them that they are only impoverishing themselves more, but even then there is always the hope that something will turn up. If they didn't bet or gamble nothing could turn up. And then all of a sudden they learned of the existence of a man who had plainly demonstrated his ability to select in advance winner after winner; not by dreams, or hocus pocus, but by the method he had adopted after years of patient study. The public always enjoyed plays and books and films about people who miraculously, or by coincidence picked the winner. But the vicar of Tapworth Magna was something quite different. And the prayer of nearly every one of his congregation was – ' Oh, please let me gain his confidence, and persuade him to tell me even just one horse a month, or (am I asking too much?) a week,' or to the like effect, when it ought to have been something very different.

The vicar looked round his congregation and began: 'My text is taken from the marriage service – "For richer for poorer, in sickness and in health, till death us do part." Till death us do part,' he repeated with emphasis.

Mrs Poulter, who was sitting fairly close to the pulpit and who had come to church for the first time for months, felt, quite wrongly (as members of a large audience, in Church or Court or elsewhere, often do) that the speaker was looking at her.

'It's a sh-shame,' she thought to herself. 'He's going to p-preach at me.' She had in mind her three husbands, all alive, all married – but none of them to her.

'My dear friends,' went on the vicar, 'it is a great pleasure to me to see this unusually large gathering and I may tell you that I am taking advantage of your presence to preach a sermon that has been long in my mind. Until today, however, there have been so few people of marriageable age present on Sundays that I have not thought it appropriate.'

'Not much to do with horses,' thought the bulk of the congregation, 'but then we weren't really entitled to expect any tips from the pulpit. After all, we've come here to get as near as possible to the vicar, to study him and find the way to his heart. We must listen intelligently and look as though we are really enjoying ourselves, in the proper spirit, of course.'

As they thought this the heads of the congregation lifted and looked at the vicar, somewhat like the heads of jurymen when they turn as one man to listen to a judge's summing up. The movement in church was slower and less like a drill movement, as befitted the occasion, but a slow motion film of it would have been most interesting. Seldom can the mind of almost a whole congregation have been so plainly revealed.

'In these days of strife and turmoil,' went on the vicar, 'it is the duty of each man and woman to foster the spirit of peace and goodwill, and that spirit can best be fostered in the home. But how can we have happy homes if the state of marriage is entered upon and discarded so lightly?'

'Happy homes,' thought the congregation, 'quite right. We must have happy homes.'

A slow-motion film would have shown a slight but definite nodding of the congregation's heads. Even Mrs Poulter took part in the movement, though there was little she knew about a happy home.

'It appals me to think that day after day hundreds of divorces take place. It is terrible.'

A gentle shaking of the head by the congregation in agreement. The sermon was more like a concerto than a solo.

'How is it to be avoided? Something must be done.'

The congregation looked determined.

'But what?'

A note of interrogation could almost be heard rising from the congregation to the rafters.

'The duties in this matter fall partly on the population as a whole and partly on the Church. Let me say quite frankly that I take a different view of those couples who have been married in a registry office from the view I take of those who have been married in church. In the former case the parties have only made promises to each other. They and the State are the parties to the marriage, and no one else. But in the latter case the Church is a party to the marriage; the husband and wife have made promises not only to each other but to their Maker, and from such a promise there can be no release except by Him to whom it was made. Though naturally I prefer that a couple should be married in church, I would far rather that they were married in a registry office if they were not completely sure that they could keep their promises. Later on, no doubt, such couples could be married again in church when they were sure of themselves. But how many people, who do get married in church, are sure of themselves?

They may think they are, but what steps have they taken to make certain? Usually none.'

The congregation looked glum.

'No steps at all,' they said to themselves. 'Disgraceful.'

'Now, what steps can they take?'

Again the rafters received the gentle note of interrogation. 'First of all, a man and woman should choose each other wisely. I do not mean that they should apply the rules which breeders of animals, dogs, cattle and horses use.'

The mention of horses brought the congregation out of its trance with a jolt.

'Horses, horses,' they said to themselves. 'Perhaps he will tell us something of his knowledge of breeding.'

A look of something like greed crept into their faces. Mrs Poulter stopped trying to remember which of her three husbands she had married in church.

'Come on, tell us something about horses,' they chanted in unison in their thoughts.

'No,' said the vicar.

The congregation relaxed with almost a sigh.

'No, but it is essential for each prospective partner to study the character of the other, to see if their respective characters are likely to harmonise. They must see each other at their worst, and often. They must go to each other's homes, and they must steel themselves against being blinded by early infatuation. Long engagements are sometimes bad, but too short engagements are far worse. Above all, they must try to imagine themselves being with each other day after day, in good times and bad, when tempers are frayed as well as when hopes are high, when money is short, when jobs are lost and when the favourite comes in a long way behind the others.'

The vicar was wont to use such expressions to hold the attention of his audience. On this occasion it had an electrifying effect. With one accord, the bulk of the congregation thought of the favourite for the Gold Vase which was shortly to be run and which happened that year to be easily the best betting race in Ascot week. Would it win?

'Yes,' said the vicar.

Thousands of imaginary pounds were staked immediately.

'Yes, these are the matters to be thought of. Not the dimple in her cheek, or his manly bearing, not her lovely voice or his leg breaks, but her inclination to jealousy and his selfishness, her sharp tongue and his forgetfulness. Ask yourselves, "Shall I be able to put up with it?" Answer honestly, and decide accordingly, and do not, I pray you, come here and ask me to marry you as though you were buying tickets for the circus. It is a glorious ceremony, that of marriage, but there is no real blessing on those who go through it without understanding all its implications and without determining that they will abide by the promises they make. The Divorce Court may be necessary for the State, but there can be no real divorce for those who are married in church till death them do part.'

The vicar completed his sermon and shortly afterwards the service ended.

It was a frequent practice of the vicar, after Sunday morning service, to call on one or other of his parishioners and have a drink and a chat before lunch. On this occasion Mrs Poulter was quite determined that she would be the parishioner concerned. As the congregation poured out of the church and joined those outside who (as at so many sporting events) had been unable to obtain admission, she took up a strategic position in the porch, through which she knew the vicar would come, and no amount of hustling or jostling could make her move. By this time there was a large number of photographers, some amateur and some professional, already taking pictures of the assembled crowd, and waiting to take the vicar as he came out. The judge made his way to the vicar's car and stood by it, and about ten minutes later he saw the vicar, and a lady whom he subsequently found to be Mrs Poulter, making towards him surrounded by a vast throng. At last they reached the car, the vicar quickly introduced him to Mrs Poulter and they got in. Eventually they managed to drive off towards Mrs Poulter's house. On looking round shortly afterwards the judge saw that they were leading a column of about twenty cars. Meanwhile Mrs Poulter was chattering.

'I'm s-so thrilled to meet you, Sir Charles,' she said. 'I wonder if it was you who gave me any of my divorces? I don't think it was, or was it? Of course, you don't remember, you have so many. Let me see, Roger was the first. You don't remember him, I suppose? Why no, of course you don't – he wasn't there. He let it go quite undefended. He deserted me, you know. Of course, he didn't really, we just separated – but then, I don't have to tell you how these things are done.'

It will be observed that when Mrs Poulter got fully into her stride she ceased to stammer.

'Raymond was the next, wasn't he, vicar?'

'My dear Mrs Poulter, you don't expect me to keep a tally for you.'

'Oh, no, vicar, if you just keep my conscience, poor wandering thing, that will be quite enough. Let me see, I was talking of Raymond. Yes, I divorced him for staying alone at an hotel in Brightbourne. He just took a double bedroom there and signed the register as "Mr and Mrs – " – now, what was the name? Oh, I remember, Knox-Bradbury – now I shouldn't have forgotten that, should I?

It was about the most innocent thing he ever did, but they gave me a divorce just the same. I remember the chambermaid, poor dear, giving evidence. She was asked if that was the lady – meaning me – whom she saw in bed the following morning. "No," she said; it was about the only truthful thing, except her name and address, that she did say in her evidence. Not that I think she meant to tell lies. But if you have a double room, and the manager shows you the register with "Mr and Mrs Knox-Bradbury" in it, it can't be very difficult for a chambermaid to remember seeing a lady. I expect you wonder why there wasn't a lady? Well, you see, there was another lady, who became a real Mrs Knox-Bradbury, but she didn't want her name mentioned in the proceedings. At the same time she didn't trust Raymond very much, and wasn't going to have him gallivanting about, even for one night, at a Brightbourne hotel. I expect she's used to it by now though. I do think it's a shame the vicar preaching that sermon at me today. Did you see him looking at me all the time? After all, I was the innocent party in each case; well, when I say innocent, I was the petitioner. I only had to ask for the discretion of the Court once. That was the last time, I think. Or was it the time before? I always mix them up. I'll tell you why. It's because one time I wanted to ask for the discretion of the Court when there wasn't any need to ask for discretion – because I wasn't actually married to anybody at the time. But it's so difficult to remember these things, and you lawyers are so particular. That's why I never quite remember when it was that I asked for the discretion that I didn't need, and when it was that I asked for the discretion that I needed very badly. I'm afraid I'm running on rather.'

She had been, and, by the time she had run down, they had reached her house. As they were getting out, the judge was horrified to see that one of the occupants of the first car behind them was the gentleman with whom he had had two beers at The Fox. It was small consolation that the gentleman was now sober. He came straight up to the judge.

'Well, well,' he said, 'where did you spring from? I couldn't make out where you'd got to the other night. You ought to have stayed. We had no end of a good time – kept it up till about three.'

Then, lowering his voice, he added: 'You've got to work pretty quickly, haven't you? How have you managed?'

For reply the judge could only think of saying: 'I found it a little close at The Fox.'

'Not half as close as you, you old oyster.'

At that moment one of Mrs Poulter's children came running up to her mother, and was immediately introduced to the judge. The journalist, still hovering nearby, nearly jumped into the air when he heard the name. By this time many more cars had driven up, and about thirty or forty people were making their way into Mrs Poulter's house. It was a pleasant party, but for the fact that Mrs Poulter was very short of gin and had to make up the deficiency with water.

Everyone who could get near enough to the vicar to speak to him, first of all told him how much they had enjoyed his sermon, and then congratulated him on the evidence he had recently given at the Old Bailey. There were two main approaches. One of them was to assume that the vicar had been lucky and that he couldn't do it again – in the hope that he would be stung into doing it again for the benefit of the questioner. To such an approach the vicar would reply by saying that he didn't think it was really luck but that it was a very trivial matter anyway, adding: 'I am glad you liked my sermon.'

The other approach was more direct: 'What have you in mind for the Gold Vase?'

'That's a race,' said the vicar, 'which interests me very much, but I haven't yet worked it out. I can say, however, that the favourite has no chance. It isn't bred for the job. It's a good-class handicapper, that's all.'

Within ten minutes of that statement having been made, the telephone exchange at Tapworth was busy putting calls through to London, giving the news that the favourite would not win the Gold Vase – with the result that by Monday those bookmakers who were offering ante-post odds on it, immediately lengthened their price, and the second favourite became a firm favourite instead. This was unfortunate for those who backed it. The vicar could have told them that that horse also was not capable of winning the race.

'You w-will tell me what's going to win, w-won't you?' said Mrs Poulter in her most wheedling voice.

'Now, Mrs Poulter,' said the vicar, 'you know quite well that I will not encourage you in your naughtiness. If I gave you the name of the winner before the race was run, I am quite sure that you would go and back it to an extent far greater than you could afford.'

'Oh, vicar,' protested Mrs Poulter, 'you've g-got me all wrong. I j-just want to have the fun of knowing what you say will win while I'm listening to the race on the wireless.'

'Oh, that's quite another matter,' said the vicar. 'You come and see me on the day of the race and I'll tell you.'

'You are sweet,' she beamed at him.

'That's quite all right,' said the vicar, 'perhaps you would like to come and listen to it with us. I shall certainly listen to it if I have the time. And it will be much more fun for you if I don't tell you until the horses are actually about to start.'

Mrs Poulter's face fell. But so quick is the human brain in emergency that in a split second she had arranged in her mind that she would go to the vicarage half an hour before the race, and would receive a telephone call from her daughter calling her urgently back. He could hardly refuse, she thought to herself, to give me the name of the horse before I go, and then I shall just have time to ring up and put the money on when I get home.

It was an excellent plan, and it would have worked out perfectly. The vicar would certainly have given her the name of the horse, and she would certainly have been able to put her money on; she would certainly have put on far too much, and she would have made a small fortune. Unfortunately, however, for reasons which will appear, the vicar was not in when she called.

CHAPTER NINE

Justice at the Races

The reason why the vicar was not in, when Mrs Poulter called on the day of the Gold Vase, was quite simple. He was at Ascot watching it, and had forgotten to put her off. Soon after her Sunday-morning party was over, the judge said that, if his work permitted it, he would like to go to Ascot on the following Tuesday. Would the vicar and his family care to join him? He offered to send a car for them. After a little thought, the vicar accepted and became quite enthusiastic about the idea. Much as he knew of racing he had never been to a horse race except the local point-to-point. But why shouldn't he go? He had no intention of making a bet, and it would be fascinating to watch some of the horses whose names and breeding he knew so well.

The judge was able to keep the engagement and, on the way to the races, the vicar explained to him something of the nature of his study of racing. Over the years he had acquired quite a considerable library and he was a regular subscriber to *Sporting Life*, *Raceform* and *The Bloodstock Breeders' Review*. He explained to the judge how much depended on breeding.

'In the Classic races, you know,' he said, 'it is usually possible to eliminate over half the final acceptors for the race, on the score of breeding. Sometimes only half a dozen horses or so are qualified by breeding to win, and I can assure you that it will be the rarest exception if a horse not qualified by breeding wins a Classic race – so rare that you can ignore the possibility. Having eliminated those who cannot win you have to judge the remainder on their known form. Sometimes it will be a little difficult to eliminate two out of the last three, but I do not normally have much difficulty in finding two, or at most three, horses one of which will win. Most years I can find the winner. So much for the Classics. As for the other races, you can do a great deal on breeding alone. Sometimes it is true that the qualities of a horse will apparently miss its son or daughter but be found in its grandson or granddaughter. Usually, however, you need not go further back than the sire and the sire of the dam. There are various rules I have been able to enunciate to which there are so few exceptions that they too can be ignored, but I will not worry you with them now.'

It was a glorious day and the whole party felt in good spirits when they arrived at the racecourse. They went into Tattersall's enclosure and bought race-cards.

'I can only tell you one horse which will win today,' said the vicar. 'Permission will win the Gold Vase. It doesn't seem to be much fancied but, barring accidents, it will win all right. The Gold Vase isn't a Classic, of course, and you don't necessarily need classic pretensions to win it, but Permission is good enough by breeding to win the St Leger and, if you look at its form closely, there's nothing wrong with it at all. I should think it had been trained for this race. But the public doesn't like horses which haven't won before. I see there's been a change of favourite, but neither the first nor second favourite can win. It is quite extraordinary that anyone can think they will. Of course, if there's an accident and two or three horses fall, anything can happen, but there are too many horses in the race for it not to be truly run, so that, all things being equal, Permission will win. I daresay it will start at 10 to 1. I shall imagine £100 on it.'

The judge did more than imagine. Making an excuse to leave the party, he went to the £5 totalisator window. He felt less embarrassed backing on the tote than with a bookmaker. With a guilty conscience (because he felt the vicar would not entirely approve – £100 was rather more than threepence) he returned to the vicar with twenty £5 tickets all on Permission in his pocket. As he rejoined them, he heard Lucy say: 'I think I'll have 10s on it.'

'You are over twenty-one,' said the vicar, 'and must do as you think fit.'

'If Lucy does, why shouldn't I?' said Caroline.

'You are over forty-one,' said the vicar, 'and should in this case do as I think fit, but, of course, I'm not stopping you.'

'Oh, very well,' said Caroline.

'Aren't you going to have a bet, Sir Charles?' asked Lucy. 'I'm going to put on 10s. Can I do anything for you?'

'That's very kind of you,' said the judge, getting out half a crown, 'perhaps you wouldn't mind putting this on for me.'

'Ten times as much as last time,' commented the vicar. 'If you went on at that rate, you'd put on twenty-five shillings next time, twelve pounds ten the next time, and a hundred and twenty-five pounds the one after. That's a lot of money.'

'This bet,' said the judge, 'is only for half a crown.'

'Hullo, father,' said a voice well known to the judge, 'I didn't know you came to these places.'

'Martin! No, I don't usually, but I've come with Mr and Mrs Meeson-Smith.'

The judge introduced his son.

'I must go and put that money on,' said Lucy.

'May I come too?' said Martin.

'Please do,' said Lucy.

Shortly afterwards the horses went down to the start.

'This is most exhilarating,' said the vicar. 'I can't think why people have to bet to enjoy it.'

The judge did not reply. He was feeling very anxious. When he had given the vicar the chance to show his skill at the Old Bailey, he was interested to know the result, but did not mind much what it was. But now he minded very much indeed, and, having put his money on, he felt less confidence in the vicar than at any previous time. The white flag was up, and, soon after, they were off. Two furlongs from home Permission started to forge ahead and the judge's excitement was great as the horse ran out a comfortable winner by two lengths.

'Well, well,' said the vicar, 'just as I thought. There, my dear, there's £1,000 in the bank of imagination for you.'

'If we had it in the National Provincial,' said his wife, 'we could have the house done up. We might even have water laid on.'

'Not to the vicarage. If we made our money in that way, I should be a spiv, not a parson. Don't you agree, Sir Charles?'

The judge was already red in the face with excitement and pleasure, so that he was unable to blush any more as he replied: 'I see your point of view, vicar. I'm sure you're right. But,' he added, 'I see Mrs Meeson-Smith's too.'

'Well done, father,' said Lucy.

'Thank you very much,' said Martin. 'Not bad at all. Now, what d'you fancy for the next race? I was thinking of Manikin.'

'The next race is much too difficult. To begin with, it's a handicap, and I don't pretend I can normally beat the handicapper. To go on with, there are a dozen horses bred to win it and none of them can be ruled out on form.'

'Well, I'm going to put half my winnings on Manikin,' said Martin. 'What about you?' And he turned to Lucy.

'You'll lose,' said Lucy, 'or you probably will. But, if you do it, I will. After all it's nice to have an interest in the race. Is Manikin bred to win it, father?'

'Oh, yes, he could win, but so could eleven others.'

'Anything for you, Sir Charles?'

'No, thank you. I prefer to keep my winnings.'

Shortly afterwards it was announced that Permission had paid 26s 6d for a win on the tote.

'That means $12^1/_4$ to 1,' said the vicar. 'You'll get your half-crown back and thirty shillings and sevenpence halfpenny as well. Better than last time. I hope it won't go to your head, Sir Charles.'

It had already done so. If you have never made a bet in your life, and never received anything which you did not earn, you will find it an astonishing sensation to receive a very large sum for doing nothing at all. The judge had won £1,225. It was stupendous. He now began to wonder how to collect the money without it being obvious. Two hundred and forty-five five-pound notes take up quite a bit of space, and they take quite a time to count.

Meanwhile Lucy had collected her winnings and returned.

'Here you are, Sir Charles,' she said, handing him his money. 'I have to thank you for an extra pound for myself. You can't put on half a crown, you know, on the tote. You could with a bookie if you had an account – but my Mr Thompson's account has been closed. So I put on an extra two shillings, sixpence for you and one and six for me. Thank you very much.'

'I must leave you for a few minutes,' said the judge. He went somewhat furtively to the paying-out windows of the tote and eventually found the £5 window. Then, rather like a small boy stealing jam, he drew his winnings; but it took quite a long time, and the next race was over before he rejoined them.

'I hope you're feeling quite well, Sir Charles,' said the vicar.

'Oh, yes, thank you,' said the judge, 'quite well. I – ' For once in his life he was at a loss for words. He did not propose to tell a direct untruth, nor indeed, even had it been true, would he have cared to say, 'I spent rather longer in the lavatory than I expected.' Fortunately, however, the vicar said the last sentence for him, in one word.

'Quite,' he said.

Manikin had won the last race and Lucy and Martin were delighted. It was their first piece of business together, in a partnership which lasted for many years. They took to each other very quickly, doing exactly the reverse of what the vicar had advised so strongly in his sermon. It is, however, revealing no secret to say that on this occasion their lack of knowledge of each other did no harm. They were, in fact, admirably suited to one another, and within two months of the Ascot meeting they were married, but a good deal happened before that – and after.

Somehow or other the judge stored his winnings about him, and he placed no more bets that day. It was lucky for him that the vicar had no more winners to give. He would not have known where to put the money. After a thoroughly enjoyable day, the judge and his party set out for home and, on the way, he managed to extract from the vicar the names of three horses which were likely to win on the following Saturday week, two at a meeting near London and one in the North.

The judge decided to attend the meeting near London and he spent a rather restless night on the Friday before it. He had learned sufficient of racing by now to know that the fact that a horse was an acceptor in a race did not necessarily mean that it would run; even the fact that its name appeared in the morning paper as a 'probable' meant no more than it said, but at any rate there was a very good hope that a 'probable' would run. Would the vicar's horses be probables? He had the most fantastic dreams on the subject. One of them went something like this.

'Might I mention to your Lordship a probable?' said counsel respectfully.

THE JUDGE: At what odds?

COUNSEL: It depends on the breeding.

THE JUDGE: A very proper observation.

COUNSEL: Who knows that you're backing it?

THE JUDGE: The vicar.

COUNSEL: You old devil, you.

THE JUDGE: You old oyster.

COUNSEL: I am very much obliged to your Lordship.

THE JUDGE: They're off.

COUNSEL: Here are the runners in the last race.

THE JUDGE: I must leave you for a moment.

COUNSEL: It is very good of your Lordship.

THE JUDGE: If it doesn't run it can't win.

COUNSEL: It's already won. The vicar's riding it.

THE JUDGE: Where do I draw my money?

COUNSEL: You don't. The vicar's against it.

THE JUDGE: I'm over twenty-one.

COUNSEL: You've won half a crown.

THE JUDGE: Lucy's a pretty girl.

COUNSEL: Is she a probable?

THE JUDGE: I want half a dozen probables, please.

COUNSEL: Will you take them with you, or could we send them for you?

THE JUDGE: Put them down to me. My name is Poulter. Sir Charles Poulter. I have three husbands.

COUNSEL: You mean wives.

THE JUDGE: When I say husbands I mean probables. Please exercise your discretion.

COUNSEL: I have used it all up.

THE JUDGE: Most probable.

Altogether it was a most uncomfortable night, and he woke a good hour before the papers arrived. As the clock slowly went round, he kept on imagining that he heard the noise of the paper-boy. The papers were due at 7.30 a.m., but he heard no sound of them at about that time. At twenty-five minutes to eight he could bear it no longer. He got up and went to the front door. No papers. The boy was late. He would be. He opened the front door, but there was no sign of him. As he closed it his housekeeper appeared.

'I was just looking for the papers,' he said rather lamely.

'I'll bring them to you as soon as they come. The boy's often late on a Saturday.'

'Thank you, Mary.'

He retired to his bedroom. He was not at all pleased with himself. The thing was getting on his nerves. Even in the war he hadn't rushed for the papers like this. Then, again, the idea of his hurrying to look at the sporting page of a newspaper was really rather dreadful. Normally he would take up *The Times*, read through the births and deaths on the front page, and go through the whole paper from cover to cover – except for the racing and those other sports in which he was not interested. Now he was going to be like those silly little men and women who wait in queues for the evening paper, and who, on getting their copy, look eagerly at the back page and stop press. He knew that he would seize the paper and look immediately for the racing. He could, of course, deliberately refrain from doing this, but that would be stupid and tantalising himself. There was a knock at the front door, and a few moments later Mary brought him the papers. He waited till she was gone, and then looked at once to see if the vicar's horses were down to run. They were, all of them, and, better still, none of them was mentioned specifically in the forecast betting – which meant that, with luck, they would run at long odds. This was by no means certain; a horse not mentioned in the forecast betting in the morning paper may run as favourite at very short odds, but it was a comfortable feeling to know that none of the racing journalists had thought of any of them.

He had decided to go alone and to have lunch on the racecourse. He took £200 in cash with him and a bag in which to carry his winnings, as he did not wish to open an account with a bookmaker or Tote Investors Ltd. He arrived in plenty of time, and although he was, of course, not a member of the race club in question, he found that by the payment of an additional fee he could become one for the day. First of all he made a general survey of the arrangements and then he bought a ticket for lunch and went into the restaurant. He sat down at an empty table for four. He had come early and not many people had arrived yet. However, shortly after he had ordered lunch a lady of between sixty-five and seventy sat down at his table. He wondered what she could be doing there, not knowing that racecourses are full of elderly ladies of between sixty-five and seventy who seem to enjoy themselves, often by themselves, very much. He had noticed at Ascot that there is no shortage of younger women, often very attractive and nearly always attractively dressed. For a high standard of good looks equally well clothed, it is difficult to beat a racecourse. A closer examination of the looks, however, normally reveals considerable hardness of character and often a fair degree of stupidity. There is really no reason why gentle, kind, intelligent and attractive women should not enjoy the spectacle of a horse race and of the people watching it, but they seldom do. It is quite unnecessary to bet. The horses in the paddock, the tiny jockeys in their brilliant colours, the running of the race, the excitement of the finish, the ingredients of the crowd, the bookmakers, tic-tac men, the very attractive girls always employed by Tote Investors Ltd, the very attractive girls not employed by Tote Investors Ltd, the look of greed, joy, and disappointment on the faces of some of the spectators according to the result, the confidential information given in hoarse (and often alcoholic) whispers behind a hand, the general atmosphere of colour and light-heartedness provide a good afternoon's entertainment for anyone. The judge missed a good deal of his, however, as he was far too interested in his object in going.

'I think it will keep fine,' said the lady.

'I hope so.'

'Last year it rained all the time.'

'How unfortunate.'

'I hear that Smashing Belle may not run. Have you heard that?'

'No, I'm afraid not.' He was relieved that Smashing Belle was not one of the vicar's horses.

'Gordon was to ride it. Pretty well a certainty with him on it, I should say.' The judge just knew enough to know that she was referring to the champion jockey, Gordon Richards.

'Indeed?'

'Oh, yes. It's just his distance. I don't think he's any good at the long-distance races. Give me Gordon in a sprint every time, I say.'

'I'm afraid I don't know very much about racing.'

'Oh, I see,' said the lady, obviously disappointed.

She raised her head, rather like a stag sniffing the wind. Then suddenly with an 'Oh … there's …' (and she mumbled a name) she got up and went over to the other end of the room, eventually sitting down at another table – also occupied by one gentleman whom she didn't know. This gentleman, however, was much more promising from her point of view. He could fairly have been described as a middle-aged racing man, which is about as offensive an expression as you could apply to anyone. A middle-aged racing man, however, would not in the least object to being so described, being far too unintelligent to appreciate the implications. The standard of intelligence among those who create the sport, the owners, trainers, jockeys, and so on, is unbelievably low, while that of the hangers-on – the middle-aged racing men – is, if possible, lower. This is no doubt one of the reasons why gentle, kind, intelligent and attractive women do not go very much to the races. They seldom associate with racing men (middle-aged or otherwise). The other day some attractive young tennis players were described in a newspaper gossip column as going out to a party in the evening. There were no men tennis players in the party, said the writer, 'which consisted of middle-aged racing men, only one of them a bachelor.' A trifle unkind this, perhaps, to the young ladies.

The judge was not long alone. Within five minutes another middle-aged to elderly lady had placed herself at his table.

'I think it will keep fine,' she said.

'I hope so.'

'Have you heard that Snorting Polly may not run?'

'No, I haven't.' Again he was relieved that it was not one of the vicar's horses.

'Gordon was going to ride it. Pretty well a certainty with him on it. Just his distance.'

'A sprint, I suppose?'

'Good gracious, no! He's no good at sprints – no better than anyone else, I mean. No, give me Gordon in a long distance, mile and a half or more, every time.'

The judge was glad that his own task was fairly simple; just to back three horses, irrespective of who was riding them. The only complication was that he had to put on a double on two horses that were running at the same time, one at the meeting where he was and one in the North. To do this he would have to approach a bookmaker, and he did not relish the prospect. He remembered the first time he had ever opened his mouth in Court as a young barrister. He now had age and experience on his side, but he felt very much in the same condition of mind as he had felt all those years before. Meanwhile he went on with his lunch and tried not to think of the ordeal before him. The room was now filling up. An elderly man, accompanied by a young and pretty girl, sat down at his table. She might have been his daughter, granddaughter, niece, grandniece or just a friend. She called him 'Spiky,' which suggested that she was in the fifth category. They drank champagne and brandy. The elderly man looked shaky and, except when the girl made him smile, miserable. The girl was bright and cheerful all the time.

'Here's fun, you old warhorse,' she said.

The elderly man made some appropriate reply, but too feebly to be heard.

'I'm going to back Bubbly till the cows come home,' said the girl.

'Bubbly,' said the old man.

'I shall make a packet.'

'Very nice,' said the old man and, raising his glass with shaking hand, sipped his drink.

'Good old Bubbly,' said the girl, 'Gordon's riding it.'

'Gordon,' said the old man.

'It's past the post.'

The old man smiled faintly. 'Past the post,' he said.

The judge felt slightly embarrassed. He called the waiter for his bill, and handed him a ten-shilling note. The bill was for half a crown.

'I'm afraid I shall have to keep you waiting for your change a bit, sir,' said the waiter.

'Oh, that'll be all right,' said the judge.

'All right, sir? Oh, thank you very much, sir. Very much obliged, sir.' And he retired with the judge's note. The judge had not the least intention of giving a tip of seven and six, but the trick was neatly done and on this strange ground he did not feel like disputing the point. He left the restaurant and wandered around. The bookmakers were now arriving in Tattersalls and putting up their stands; the public were coming in large numbers and there was a general atmosphere of bustle and expectation. As two o'clock approached he went into Tattersalls and looked at the various bookmakers. He was anxious to find one who was offering to lay bets for the northern meeting. He soon spotted one. After a little hesitation he approached him.

'Would you take a double for both meetings?'

'The first race?'

'No, the four o'clock at each.'

'Not now. I'll take it later when we've got the runners.'

It was something to know that he could place the bet, and the judge made a mental note of the name and position of the bookmaker.

The other horse recommended by the vicar was running in the three o'clock. The first race was at two-thirty and he was able to watch it with interest but without excitement. As soon as it was over and the runners for the three o'clock had been announced, he went to the £5 tote windows and invested (as they euphemistically call it) £100 on Maiden Aunt. As he was actually handing the money through the window, an announcement through the loudspeaker gave him a very nasty shock. It was just this: 'Will Mr Justice Painswick please come to the office of the Clerk of the Course.'

The speaker repeated it. The judge felt as though a heavy hand had suddenly been laid on his shoulder. This is just what a thief about to put his ill-gotten gains on a horse, must feel like when the hand of the policeman descends upon him, he thought. He hastily took his twenty tickets and made his way to the office. He could not imagine why he was wanted. He had no near relatives except his son, and only his housekeeper knew where he was. Perhaps Martin had had an accident and she had told them where he was. Perhaps his flat had been broken into. He could not think of any other possible explanations. As a matter of fact the original, though not the immediate cause, of his being required was the throwing of an alarm clock, some five years previously, by Emily Trent at the head of her husband, William. It had hit him. Up till that moment, although they had their quarrels, he had never been in the least violent. In the ensuing four and a half years, however, he made up for his previous gentleness. He retaliated strongly in respect of the alarm clock, and this started a habit. His wife kept her end up as well as possible, but he was much stronger than she was and, though she thought of poison, she was too frightened of the consequences (to herself) to use it. There was no other method of fighting at which he was not her superior. It was not, therefore, altogether surprising that four and a half years after the alarm clock incident the case of *Trent v Trent* appeared in the Divorce Court list of defended cases, each party seeking a divorce from the other on the ground of cruelty. The reader may fairly ask, however, what possible connection this can have with Mr Justice Painswick and his visit to a racecourse near London. This will appear soon. In due course the case of *Trent v Trent* was heard. Mr Commissioner Pink, who tried the case, announced his decision at the end of a long judgment. He said there had been faults on both sides. He believed the husband on this and the wife on that. He disbelieved the husband on one dispute, he disbelieved the wife on another. There was this to be said for the husband, there was that to be said for the wife. There had not been sufficient give and take between the parties. He doubted the flat-iron incident. The wife's mother was a prejudiced witness. So was the husband's sister. He found as a fact that the wife had not been thrown downstairs – she had slipped. He found as another fact that the wife had slapped her husband's face, not very hard, but quite hard enough to hurt him, enough to anger him. He had then made her nose bleed. He should not have done so. There was not enough mutual understanding between the parties. The husband drank too much on occasions. The wife nagged him sometimes. On the whole, he accepted the wife's evidence about the walk in the park, but he thought she exaggerated this matter. The wife had started it, the husband had finished it. It was a difficult case, but on the whole, by and large, doing the best he could, taking all the circumstances into consideration and bearing in mind everything that had been said (so very ably) by learned counsel (to both of whom he was very much indebted) he was going to find (not without some hesitation and realising that another judge might have taken a different view – but he could only do the best he could – and he was not forgetting the evidence of the dustman or any of the other evidence for that matter) he was going to find in favour of the wife.

Accordingly, Mrs Trent obtained a decree nisi of divorce. If the reader is still there, he is presumably waiting to know how all this is connected to the judge at the races. This will appear very soon.

Until they eventually separated before the divorce proceedings, Mr and Mrs Trent and the three children lived in five rooms on the two upper floors of a house in London. Before the proceedings started Mr Trent left his wife and children in sole possession of their five rooms. Although he left them there, however, Mr Trent claimed to be the tenant. During the divorce proceedings he had from time to time come to the premises, avowedly to collect some of his property, but in fact to make himself a nuisance. He succeeded in the latter direction to such an extent that his wife applied to and obtained an injunction from the Divorce Court ordering him not to molest her pending the determination of the proceedings and in particular not to go to the house where she lived. This put an end to the nuisance for the moment, but as soon as Mrs Trent had her decree made absolute, the injunction against

Mr Trent automatically lapsed. When he discovered this, Mr Trent started coming round to the house again, and although he did not create a breach of the peace or court police interference, he did everything else to annoy his former wife. Finally, he did something much more than annoying. He told his wife to leave the five rooms with their three children (of which she had the custody). 'Where to?' said his wife. The reply was not in polite language, but the effect of it was that Mr Trent did not exactly care where she and the children went.

'You asked for their custody,' he said, 'and you've got it. All right, go and custody them, but outside this house. This is mine, see. I'm the tenant. You can go to the workhouse, or chuck yourself into the river or under a bus, or you can just walk up and down the Embankment until you get tired. All you're not going to do is stay here, see? This is my place, and you're going out of it, see?' And he put his unpleasant face far nearer than was necessary to enable her to smell the beer.

'Who says you're the tenant? We're both the tenants.'

'Oh, no we're not – clever. I've been looking at the rent book, see, and I'm the tenant.'

He had indeed been looking at the rent book; whether he had been doing any more than look is a subject which had to be investigated subsequently, but the decision on the matter doesn't concern this story. No doubt this prompts the reader to enquire again what any of this has to do with Mr Justice Painswick. This will appear extremely soon.

Now the landlord of Mr Trent (or of Mr and Mrs Trent as the case may be) was a friend of Mr Trent, and when Mrs Trent persisted in saying that her husband was not the sole tenant and refused to move out into the street with the three children, he gave Mr Trent permission to take the law into his own hands. Mr Trent accordingly started to build a door at the bottom of the staircase leading up to the five rooms. He informed Mrs Trent that he alone would have the key, and that unless she stayed in the house for the rest of her life, she would find herself effectively locked out. Mr Trent started to put his threat into operation, and, as soon as he began to make the door, Mrs Trent rushed off to her solicitors. Her solicitors immediately issued a writ against Mr Trent, and they drew an affidavit for Mrs Trent to swear, in which was set out, in language which she did not fully understand, the threats and actions of her ex-husband and the statement that, unless Mr Trent was ordered by the Court to cease his activities at once, Mrs Trent and the children would find themselves in the street.

Now the law's delays are proverbial and the law is sometimes very slow, too slow. But in a case of emergency the law can act with extreme rapidity. At any hour of the day or night, in term time and vacation time, any urgent application can be heard by a judge either at the Law Courts or at his house, or on a golf course or wherever he may happen to be; and in proper cases a judge will make an order to prevent irremediable harm from being done. Normally, in the King's Bench Division of the High Court of Justice this jurisdiction is exercised by a judge called the 'Chambers Judge.' He is available day and night somewhere, and his address is known to the authorities. Now Mr Justice Painswick was not Chambers Judge on the day in question. If he had been, he would not have gone to the races, for fear that the very thing might happen which did, in fact, happen to him. So what the quarrel between Mr and Mrs Trent has to do with the judge will positively now appear. The Chambers Judge for the day was taken ill, and the only judge who could be found near

London was Mr Justice Painswick. The authorities at the Law Courts found out from his housekeeper where he was, and accordingly, solicitor and counsel, armed with writ and affidavit, went post-haste to the racecourse and enquired for him. They could hardly have come at a more inconvenient moment. In the first place, he wanted to watch the race; secondly, and even more important, he had to put on his money for the two races at four o'clock. When he had learned why he had been summoned to the office, he was extremely worried lest either the hearing of the matter would take so long that he wouldn't be able to place his bets in time, or that he would have to excuse himself in the middle for the purpose of making them. When there is added to this his continuous excitement during most of the meeting, due to his object in going there, it is not unnatural that the normally genial judge was not so hearty in his welcome of Mr Satterthwaite of Counsel and Mr Coke, the solicitor instructing him. However, when the Clerk of the Course had brought them to him and been kind enough to provide them with a fairly quiet corner in which to deal with the matter, he did his best to appear normal.

'My Lord,' began Mr Satterthwaite, 'I am extremely sorry to have to trouble your Lordship, but the learned Chambers Judge is ill and your Lordship is the only judge we could find. As the matter is extremely urgent, I hope your Lordship will hear us and forgive the interruption of your Lordship's enjoyment.'

The judge did not care very much for this expression, but he only said: 'If it is really urgent, I will hear it.'

'I assure your Lordship that I shouldn't have dreamed of troubling your Lordship if it hadn't been urgent.'

'They are under starter's orders,' said the loudspeaker.

'It's a shame to spoil your Lordship's sport,' said Mr Satterthwaite, 'I do apologise.'

'Will you kindly show me the writ and affidavit,' said the judge, controlling his voice as much as possible, but it was not easy.

'If your Lordship pleases. This is a claim by an ex-wife against her ex-husband for an injunction to prevent him from throwing her and three young children … three young children, my Lord – '

'I heard you the first time,' said the judge. 'Your Lordship's sport' still rankled.

'If your Lordship pleases, from throwing them into the street pending the determination of the dispute between – '

'They're off,' interrupted him.

Mr Satterthwaite paused for a moment, and into his whole face came an expression of genuine concern for the judge. He said nothing, but his looks said so plainly, 'So very, very sorry to interfere with your Lordship's sport,' that the judge only just realised that he hadn't said a word.

'What are you waiting for?' he said, with some asperity.

'So sorry, my Lord. Someone's losing a lot of money now. Forgive me, my Lord, I was saying that the defendant is about to throw the plaintiff and her children in the street. I'm asking your Lordship for an *ex parte* injunction to prevent this until the Court decides who is entitled to the tenancy of the premises. The ex-husband claims to be the tenant, the ex-wife says they are joint tenants. The husband is trying to take the law into his own hands. The wife has been in possession since the divorce proceedings started. He could have brought an action for possession. Instead of that, as your Lordship will see, he is starting to make a door which will effectively prevent the plaintiff from getting in once she has gone out. My Lord, the divorce petition was on the ground of cruelty and his conduct is entirely consistent with the findings of the learned Commissioner who granted her a decree on that ground.'

'That is pure prejudice,' said the judge. 'The only questions are – '

As he began the sentence, he heard the loudspeaker starting to give the result of the last race. 'First – '

He could not avoid pausing momentarily, but he quickly went on, and in consequence drowned in his own ears almost the whole of the remainder of the announcement.

Maiden Aunt was number 21 on the card. He just heard the announcer say 'First, number twenty – ' but he could not hear whether he left it at twenty or went on to add one, two or three. Of course, Mr Satterthwaite could have told him.

'The only questions are – one, have you made out a *prima facie* case that the plaintiff has an interest in the tenancy; two, should the *status quo* be preserved until the trial?'

'Well, my Lord, at the moment it will only be until the writ and summons are served on the defendant. I only want an injunction till Tuesday. I ask your Lordship's leave to issue and serve a summons for that day.'

'Quite right, Mr Satterthwaite.' The judge paused a moment, and then looked again at the affidavit. 'Yes,' he said, 'I think you may have an order till Tuesday. The husband has somewhere to live. It cannot possibly do him any harm to wait till Tuesday. Very well, then.'

He wrote his order on the affidavit, initialled it and handed back the papers to counsel.

'Thank you very much, my Lord. I'm so very grateful to your Lordship for having dealt with the matter. Your

Lordship sees it was very urgent. Thank you so much, my Lord. I hope your Lordship has a good day.'

'Good afternoon,' said the judge, and walked away as though he were in no hurry at all. In fact, he wanted to run. At last he found the result. He had won again. It was really incredible. The vicar had now announced in advance six successive winners, and no losers – four in Court, one at Ascot, and one now. Later on the tote returns were announced and he found that he had won just over £600. Altogether now he had made getting on for £2,000. He didn't, however, propose to lose all this in the next two races. Punctually at 3.30 he presented himself at the stand of the bookmaker who had promised to lay him the double. Both these horses were running, and still as outsiders. He decided to put £50 on the double and £100 on each horse separately. If they both won, he would have made all he needed. The bookmaker looked at him when he heard the amount he wished to stake, but he took the bet.

'The double at SP,' he said.

'I beg your pardon?' said the judge.

'At SP,' repeated the bookmaker.

Now, normally, as a judge, he had no hesitation in asking the meaning of anything he did not fully understand, but this time he said, 'Thank you,' took his ticket and beat a retreat without quite knowing what had happened.

However, it did not take him very long to discover that his bet on the double was at starting price, while his single bets were at 20 to 1 and 14 to 1 respectively. He was quite satisfied. If starting price were no worse than that, he would make about £19,000 altogether, which, together with his past winnings, would be enough for Martin. He realised that the price might be a little better or a little worse, but it was almost bound to be near enough what he required. He had already been told that bookmakers in Tattersalls were quite safe and that there was no fear of his being welshed. His confidence in the vicar was now becoming almost unbounded. The fact that both horses were outsiders and were, in the opinion of their trainers and the public, unlikely to win, meant nothing to him. The vicar had said they would win – they would win. The only slight doubts he had about the matter were when he realised how much it meant to him to win. It was too good to be true. At last the horses went down to the start. Hazelnut was his horse. It had a small boy as a jockey. The race was a long one, two miles. Hazelnut started as a complete outsider; no one thought it would win, except the vicar and the judge. Even the few others who backed it thought they had lost their money. Some chose it by accident because the price was a good one; the trainer put a few pounds on it just for luck; the owner did nothing about it beyond saying to the small boy, 'Go to the front and stay there.' He never thought he would be able to stay there. The handicapper (this was one of the rare occasions when the vicar thought he could beat him) certainly didn't think he could win. He gave him very little weight and the allowance for the little boy apprentice made it still less. They were off. Hazelnut went to the front at once. Not only did he stay there, but he went so far ahead that the crowd laughed. No one thought he would win. It would be the usual tale, and, on coming into the straight or earlier, Hazelnut would fold up and eventually come in last.

'He can never keep it up,' they said. But as the boy continued to hold his lead, and even to increase it, the laughter stopped, and a buzz of surprise sprang up instead. Half a mile from home he was leading by a clear eighteen lengths. Now, instead of 'He'll never do it,' 'They'll never catch him,' started to be heard. The cry of 'They'll never catch him' is very frequently ill-founded, but, as the horses got nearer and nearer to the winning-post, it seemed to be nearer and nearer to the truth. Two furlongs from home it was obvious that, unless the small boy fell off or the horse fell down or some similar accident occurred, Hazelnut was bound to win, and, to the cheers of the crowd – hardly any of whom had backed it and nearly all of whom were losers – Hazelnut cantered in a winner by ten lengths.

The judge's excitement was now almost more than he could bear. Nothing he could do could control it. Outwardly it only showed in the redness of his face. Inwardly it was terrible. He kept on telling himself: 'Behave yourself. You're a High Court judge. Where is your dignity now? You must not get so excited. It's indecent. Think of the times when, from the bench, you've spoken of gamblers with a pitying or sardonic smile. Do you remember saying to the jury, with such a smile, "Whether or not you avail yourselves of Mr Meeson-Smith's hints is entirely a matter for you"?' But the only reply he could make was: 'I can't help it.' And now he was waiting for the result from the northern meeting. In any event, even if that horse lost, he had made £2,000. Then he reminded himself that that would be nothing like enough, and, that unless the double came off, he would have to go to another meeting, and possibly more than one. He certainly did not want to do so. He realised that he might get entertainment from an occasional visit as a non-betting spectator. But he made up his mind that he would never bet again, once Martin was out of trouble. In any event, he didn't need the money. He had no other responsibilities and his judge's salary was ample for him. Although he now felt almost certain that the vicar's horse would win in the North, he waited in an agony of suspense for the result. And at last it came. Tomahawk – his horse – had won at 100 to 6. He worked out his winnings roughly. They were certainly well over £20,000. He had done it. But what a huge sum to take away. Perhaps the bookmaker would want to give him a cheque? Would that be safe? It might be dishonoured. There was no legal liability on him to honour it. Perhaps it would be better to have the cash. Even a big bookmaker, he thought, might decide to default for such a large sum, certainly after he'd left the racecourse. Yes, he'd have it in cash.

He went up to the bookmaker as quietly as he could, with his ticket. The bookmaker was not at all pleased.

'You'll have to wait for your double,' he said. 'I'll pay the singles now.'

'Gosh, you've had a bit of something luck,' said the bookmaker's clerk, as he started to count out the amount the judge had won on the single bets, between £3,000 and £4,000.

As he received the money, the judge kept saying to himself: 'Now this really is happening. I am really getting the money. It isn't a dream, and he's able to pay me and I'm being paid.'

The last race was over by the time he had been paid.

'You'll have to wait till I've done the others,' said the bookmaker, 'or will you take a cheque?'

'I'd prefer cash,' said the judge.

'Well, you'll have to wait.'

'Very well, but I hope you won't be too long.'

'I'll be as long as I something well like, you something, something, something,' said the bookmaker. He had lost a lot of money, and he didn't like it at all.

Whether he would have said all that, if he had realised to whom he was talking will never be known, but, in view of his losses, he would probably have said that he didn't mind if he was the something Lord Chancellor and Lord Chief Justice all rolled into one.

It was not very pleasant for the judge to be shouted at, but there was not much he could do about it. He made one attempt.

'There's no need to be abusive,' he said quietly.

'You something son of a something, I'll say what I something well like.'

The judge could have said that he would report him to the authorities, to which, no doubt, the bookmaker would have replied with extreme blasphemy. However, the judge did not relish the idea at all of making a complaint. His only desire was to get away as soon as possible. At last everything else was done, and the bookmaker turned to the judge.

'And now for your something double. How much d'you want?'

'I haven't exactly worked it out,' said the judge, 'but – '

'Well, something well work it out, if you want your money.'

'Very well,' said the judge. 'It'll take me a minute or two.' He had learned from the vicar how to do the sum.

'Something well hurry up. I can't stay here all night.'

After a few minutes the judge said: 'I make it £18,500 exactly.'

'What the something hell are you talking about?' said the bookmaker.

'Well,' said the judge, 'Tomahawk won at 100 to 6, and Hazelnut at 20 to 1, and I had £50 on, I may have made a mistake. I'll do it again.'

'Do it again? What the something hell d'you think you're doing?'

'Working it out.'

'I'll do it with you,' said the bookmaker.

'The double was £50. That right, Nobby?' and he turned to his assistant.

'That's right, £50.'

'Right, cock. You've got exactly £2,000 to come, and that's 2,000 something pounds too much.'

'Nonsense,' said the judge. 'My arithmetic may have been wrong, but it's not as wrong as all that.'

'Your something arithmetic,' said the bookmaker.

It is interesting to compare this conversation with the occasions in Court when sums had to be worked out. With a gentle smile Mr Justice Painswick would say: 'Well, I make it £270 5s 4d, but I expect my arithmetic is wrong. It usually is.'

His arithmetic was not usually wrong; it was usually right, but it is a normal habit of most judges to pretend that they can't add or subtract once they get into three figures.

'No, your Lordship is absolutely right. My learned friend agrees.'

'How nice to be right for once.'

Much bowing and scraping and exchanging of compliments, very respectful by counsel, very genial by the judge. On this occasion it was rather different.

'Your something arithmetic.' Surely several ushers will rush up and throw the man into jail. But not a bit of it, he continued to hurl abuse at the judge and to bring his face nearer to the judge's. There was not much difference in the colour, but the bookmaker had the advantage of being a heavy drinker of long standing, and there was permanence behind his redness. For the moment, however, the judge's certainly held its own. Excitement, anger and frustration effectively pumped the blood to his head and kept it there.

'Now, look here, cock,' went on the bookmaker, 'I've got a book of rules, see, and when you bet with me you bet on those rules, see, and if you don't like those rules you can bet with someone else, see, and anyway, you can take your something bets to some other something bookmaker next time, see.'

'But what has this to do with it?'

'My rules say that there's a limit of 40 to 1 on a double when the races are at the same time. Want to see 'em?'

'Yes,' said the judge, 'I do.'

'Show the something the something rules, Nobby.'

'It's quite right, mister,' said Nobby, who was a polite little man. 'Here they are.'

He held in his hand the little book, and there was no doubt but that Rule 23 said what the bookmaker had stated.

'I have never seen these before,' said the judge.

'Well, you've seen them now,' said the bookmaker.

'You ought to have told me before I placed the bet.'

'Bring your something nanny with you next time. You could have asked. Ought to have told you? My something grandmother.'

The judge had in mind what the position would be between ordinary contracting parties. In such a case the bookmaker would have been quite clearly in the wrong. But a bet is a very different thing. There is no legal liability, anyway. The only question was whether Tattersalls would uphold the bookmaker. Undoubtedly he had the rule in his little book. It would be bad enough to refer the matter to Tattersalls at all, but to refer it to them and lose would be dreadful. Although he saw his hopes crashing to the ground, he felt he would have to make the best of it. After all, he had won quite a lot. Not enough for Martin, but a very substantial start. Well, he would have to go to another meeting, that was all, and make up the rest.

'Do you something well want the money, or not?' asked the bookmaker.

'Very well,' said the judge. 'I'll take the £2,000.'

'That's all you're something well going to get, and you're something lucky to get that. Some something people don't know when they're something well off.'

The counting out of the money was a considerable ordeal to the judge in all the circumstances, but eventually it ended. When it was all over, the bookmaker held out his hand.

'No hard feelings, mate,' he said, 'but you've something well cost me a packet.'

The judge shook hands and left, but it is doubtful if such a substantial winner has ever, in the history of racing, left a racecourse in such an unpleasant frame of mind, which was very little improved by the bookmaker's friendly gesture.

CHAPTER TEN

A Stroke

While the judge was at the races, Lucy and Martin were having a walk in the country.

'You know,' said Martin, 'I'm getting to like you a good deal.'

'Snap,' said Lucy.

'If you really mean that, there's a lot you ought to know about me before we finish the hand.'

'I'm all attention.'

'Mind you, I'm not telling you this out of any twinge of conscience or moral sense. It's just that, if we happened to go ahead as we've started, it would be infernally awkward later on if you didn't know.'

'Tell me the worst.'

'I can't. I expect that's to come. Now you probably imagine that I'm the respectable son of a highly respectable father, and that, even if I don't inherit my father's intelligence, I do inherit his integrity. Well, the first point is, I don't. It's a very curious thing but, whereas my father would never dream of doing anything which could be considered by the most fastidious person as in the least degree dishonest – he is a typical English judge, and is even honest intellectually – I, on the other hand would do much more than dream of doing dishonest things.'

'How often have you been to prison?'

'It's no good joking about it. I haven't yet, but there's a very strong possibility that I shall.'

'Why?'

'Because my methods of making money – which, by the way, I like to have in as large quantities as possible, are often, not always, contrary to the criminal law. By the way, when I say I like to have money I only want it for what it will do. I like to live comfortably and enjoy myself. It can't be done without money. I'm beginning to feel it can't be done without you.'

'What am I supposed to do while you're in prison? Will you make me an allowance?'

'Oh, good heavens, no, you'll be living on what's left of my ill-gotten gains.'

'It sounds quite exciting. And we oughtn't to get bored with each other, either. That's what breaks up so many marriages. (I take it that was your for once honourable intention?) Looking at the same face behind the same paper every day of the week. Hearing the same silly remarks. Listening to the same complaints and, worse still, when other people are about, hearing the same jokes, with no intervals for rest and refreshment. Now, if you oblige by going to prison every so often, we shall not get bored with each other and it will be so exciting when you come out.'

'I hope you're serious about it, because I am.'

'Never more so. You're just my type. I'm sure I could live with you very happily – on and off, if necessary.'

They said much more on the same lines, but, behind the flippancy, there was growing very fast between these two a deep and abiding affection, which, in fact, lasted all their lives.

A few days later Martin called on his father and received a considerable shock when the judge told him he could let him have £10,000.

'But that's marvellous. It's really terribly good of you.'

'Will that be enough?'

'Well, it should help to keep things going for a bit. It won't stop the landslide though, if I don't find the balance, the creditors say they'll compound for two-thirds and not a penny less; £10,000 is about one-third. If we pay that down, I expect they'd give us a month or so to find the rest. They won't give us much longer, though. They want our blood, if they can't get two-thirds of their money. But thanks ever so much. It's really too good of you. I won't ask how you got it.'

'You know quite well how I got it. But I suppose I shall have to get some more the same way. But why on earth should I? You can. Yes, that's the idea. I'll see the vicar, and – '

'I'm afraid that's out of the question. The poor old boy's had a stroke. I meant to tell you at once, but you got in first with your £10,000.'

The judge's heart had started to beat very fast. This was the end then. It was hopeless now. Then, with a shock, he realised that he was much more concerned about his own affairs than about the vicar and his wife and daughter.

'Poor chap,' he said, 'how is he?'

'Not too bad, but he can't speak, and they have to be very careful in case he has another. With luck, though, they say he'll pull through, but it'll take some time.'

'I suppose he'll have to retire?'

'I imagine so, but I don't know what they'll live on. If he retires, they'll have to give up the house, and his pension will be terribly small. I've been talking to Lucy about it. By the way, we're going to get married.'

'But you've only known her about three weeks.'

'Some people have known each other for years and made a mess of it just the same. We shan't get married for a month or so, but I think it'll work out.'

'It won't work out if you go to prison on your honeymoon. How are you going to get the other £10,000?'

'Oh, you never know. I'll have a try, anyhow. And I can't tell you how grateful I am. How did you like it, by the way?'

'I think,' said the judge, 'we won't discuss that.'

Meanwhile at the vicarage at Tapworth Magna the vicar's affairs had considerably improved. His physical condition was about the same, but his prospects of recovering were certainly enhanced by the turn of events. The Bishop had called to see his wife, and was surprised to find the door opened by a parlourmaid. He was still more surprised to find an excellent nurse in attendance. He had not recovered from the shock when Mrs Meeson-Smith came out of her husband's room and took him into the drawing-room.

'I am terribly sorry,' he said, 'I knew he had high blood pressure, but I had no idea that it was so bad. How is he today?'

'Fairly comfortable, thank you. It is so very kind of you to come, and I do want to have a chat with you.'

'How can I help?'

'Wellsby will have to retire, of course.'

'Oh, it's early days to speak of that.'

'No, I'm quite sure of it, and I want to get things settled for him so that he needn't worry.'

'Naturally. Now do tell me what I can do. You can be assured that anything in my power will be done.'

'You are very kind. Wellsby would be as grateful as I am. Now it's quite obvious that the new vicar isn't going to live here, isn't it?'

'Well,' said the Bishop, 'well, that may be. But, of course, in any event we shouldn't dream of asking you to go until your husband is quite fit to be moved. Don't disturb yourself on that point. Of course, the pension is very small, but I suppose you will be able to find somewhere – '

His voice trailed off as he wondered how they would, in fact, be able to find a place at a rent they could afford and to eat as well.

'I was wondering,' said Caroline, 'how much the Commissioners would want for the vicarage, if we bought it?'

The Bishop was thunderstruck. The Meeson-Smiths had no money whatever. What was the meaning of it? Suddenly, an unpleasant thought came to his mind. He had, of course, heard about the vicar and the horses. Could it be that all the time he had been backing horses himself? He couldn't believe it. And what a hypocrite the man must have been. It couldn't be so. He would have staked his reputation on the honesty of mind and purpose of the vicar. Yet, how else could they buy the vicarage? And what about the maid and the nurse?

'If you could let us have it fairly cheaply, I thought we might get water laid on. They've got it as far as Clark's farm already. And electricity is not too far away.'

'I'm very pleased to hear of your good fortune,' said the Bishop, rather uncomfortably. 'It has come at a most opportune time, if I may say so.'

'It has, indeed. I must show you the letter.'

'Letter?'

'Yes, I'll get it.' She went over to a desk and took out a letter which she handed to the Bishop. It was from a firm of solicitors. It ran as follows:

Dear Madam,

Our client, who desires to remain anonymous, has long been an admirer of your husband and deeply regrets to hear of his severe illness. He hopes that recovery will come soon and be complete. In the meantime, he realises how difficult is the situation which you will have to face and he would like, if you will allow him, to be of some assistance in the matter. It has often struck our client how unfortunate it is that the two most important professions in the world, that of the parson and the schoolmaster, are the worst paid. He feels strongly that, if these professions had been the most sought after by men of integrity and intelligence during the last hundred years, the deplorable lack of understanding which obtains among all classes of the community today would not exist. If, however, it had been suggested in 1850 that two shillings should be put on income tax for the purpose of education, our client is sure that his grandfather (an eminent and successful barrister) would have been appalled and called it something like anarchy. Our client appreciates that, had he himself lived then instead of now, he might well have thought the same. All he can now do is to express his views whenever he gets the chance and in proper cases give assistance to the members of those professions who most need it. Our client is a wealthy man and it gives him the greatest pleasure when he is allowed to render this service. He sincerely trusts that this will be one of the occasions of his pleasure and, in the strong hope that you will see fit to accept it, he has instructed us to send you the enclosed cheque. May we expect the pleasure of a favourable reply at your earliest convenience and express the hope that your husband's health will soon be fully restored.

We are, Madam,

Yours faithfully,

PENNYLOVE AND DREWITT.

'Dear me,' said the Bishop, 'how very kind. Have you any idea who it can be? Possibly the Anstruthers, but I shouldn't have thought so.'

'It doesn't sound like them.'

'I oughtn't to be inquisitive, but, in view of the suggestion that you might buy the house, I wondered – '

Caroline interrupted him.

'£15,000,' she said.

'Good gracious,' said the Bishop, and just for one fleeting moment he thought of his own means.

'You'll accept it, I hope.'

'I have already done so, without even trying to ask Wellsby. I think it was my duty. He has served the Church and his parish to the very best of his ability for years and without sparing himself in any way. Now he needs the help and I think I should be very wrong to refuse it. Don't you agree, Bishop?'

'I do, Mrs Meeson-Smith, I do. It is a very large sum, but I feel sure that it will be better in your and your husband's hands than in many others. I am delighted at the news and I do so very much hope that he will soon be able to take active advantage of it.'

'I'm so glad you agree,' said Caroline. 'I want to tell my husband when he's well enough. You will back me up, won't you?'

'Yes, I will,' said the Bishop. 'Yes, I will. And now about the house, I'll have enquiries made to see what the position is, but I have little doubt but that the price will be well within your reach. It is no longer rude to mention such things, but the lack of repair and lack of amenities – '

'Talking of amenities,' said Caroline, 'do let me give you a glass of sherry or a whisky and soda.'

'That is very kind. A glass of sherry would be very nice.'

Not long afterwards the Bishop took his leave. He was delighted. He had a great regard for the Meeson-Smiths; the husband, the almost perfect country parson, loved and respected by his folk, broadminded but with a very definite set code of conduct from which he never swerved; he must have had his faults, but they were difficult to find; Caroline, the almost perfect wife of the country parson, always smiling, very hard-working, never too tired to help; a loving wife and mother; she, too, must have had her faults, but they were equally hard to find. What a Godsend it was that the money had come as it did. The Bishop was a good and kind man and his heart was overflowing with joy as he went home to give the news to his wife, who had been at school with Caroline. She, also, was delighted, but he could not at first understand her immediate reaction on being told the news.

'Clever girl,' she had said. But, although he did not quite understand at first, on reflection he did not ask for an explanation.

CHAPTER ELEVEN

Painswick (Junior) v Gloster (First Round)

It soon became apparent that, unless Martin and his partner could raise another very substantial sum of money, they would be put into bankruptcy and their affairs investigated with unpleasant thoroughness.

The result of such investigation would almost certainly be a prosecution.

Martin thought hard for a number of days. Then he wrote a letter to America and, after he had had a reply, he walked into the offices of one of the best known firms of solicitors in the City, Messrs Broadacre, Barley and Merryweather.

'I would like to see one of the partners,' he told a clerk in the outer office. 'My name is Martin Painswick. I am a son of Mr Justice Painswick and I want to consult your firm about an action I wish to bring.'

Normally a firm of this standing would only deal with a new client upon a suitable introduction. However, the son of a High Court judge is a different matter. At that time nothing was known publicly against him, and accordingly he was soon shown into the office of Mr Merryweather. They shook hands.

'I understand you are a son of Mr Justice Painswick.'

'That's right,' said Martin. 'I expect you know my father.'

'Not personally, but our firm have often had cases tried before him.'

'I hope you were satisfied.'

'If I may respectfully say so, your father is a very great judge.'

'Thank you very much. I've always heard so.'

'Now what is it we can do for you? I understand you want to bring an action against someone.'

'That's right,' said Martin, 'I'll tell you about it.'

He then proceeded to explain to Mr Merryweather the nature of the action he wanted to bring. The more he said, the less Mr Merryweather liked it, but a High Court judge is a very important person from any solicitor's point of view, however reputable and distinguished the solicitor, and Mr Merryweather decided to go on listening.

However, after about half an hour he came to a definite decision in the matter.

'I'm afraid,' he said, 'that this really isn't the sort of case we do.'

'Oh dear,' said Martin, 'I thought you did a lot of litigation.'

'That's quite true, but your case isn't quite in our line.'

Mr Merryweather thought for a moment.

'I tell you what I can do, though. There's an extremely able young man I know who's in practice on his own. I can thoroughly recommend him, and, if you like, I'll telephone and ask if he can see you.'

'That will be very kind,' said Martin, 'though, of course, I should have preferred to have your firm.'

Mr Merryweather thereupon telephoned to Mr Gordon Huntley, and arranged an appointment for Martin for the same day. As soon as Martin had gone, however, he telephoned Mr Huntley again.

'Look here,' he said, 'I don't want to say too much, and

I may be quite wrong, but I don't care for this thing very much. Don't take it on if you don't want it, but look out if you do.'

Mr Huntley thanked Mr Merryweather and said he would suspend judgment until he had seen Martin.

The interview with Mr Huntley did not last very long. He was a young and able solicitor and an extremely scrupulous one.

He wanted new clients and, on the face of it, the son of a High Court judge would be an admirable client; but, even if he had not been warned by Mr Merryweather, he would have refused to take on the case.

He did not wish to turn Martin away without doing something for him, however, and he in turn telephoned to Messrs Braggs, Golightly and Sharpe.

That firm did not, in fact, contain a Braggs, a Golightly or a Sharpe; and although its notepaper stated that it incorporated Hugg, Neadham and Charlesmith, its sole proprietor was a Mr Harold Spratt.

Mr Huntley knew Mr Spratt to be a moderately able and industrious solicitor, anxious to get as much business as possible, and fairly considered in the profession to be sharp.

That was not to say that he did anything that was likely to be discovered as dishonest or unprofessional. He was too clever for that.

Those who were against him, however, had to look out for themselves, or they were likely to be outsmarted. He was not too particular what kind of work he took on, provided he was sure of his money. That was indispensable, but, given that, there was hardly a case he would refuse.

If it looked a little disreputable on arriving at his office, he dressed it up nicely before it went into Court, washed its hands, combed its hair, and, if necessary, gave it an almost entirely new suit.

Mr Huntley rightly thought that Mr Martin Painswick and Mr Spratt were admirably suited to each other as client and solicitor. And client and solicitor they duly became.

'Come in, Mr Painswick,' said Mr Spratt at their first interview.

'I hope I shall be able to be of service to you. I know your father well, only as a judge, of course. A fine judge, should go to the Court of Appeal. You're not in the law, I gather?'

'No, I did start to read for the Bar, but I gave it up and became an accountant.'

'Well, now what's the trouble?'

'I've got a claim against Frank Gloster, the MP, you know.'

'What for?'

'Commission on a deal. Introduced him to someone who introduced him to someone who introduced him to someone at the Ministry of Supply. Surplus goods, you know. Going very cheap. He made the hell of a profit, and now he won't pay.'

'What was the agreement?'

'Well, he said he'd see me all right if it went through.'

'How d'you know it did go through?'

'Well, I happened to meet a chap who bought some of the goods from Gloster's people.'

'Gloster didn't buy them himself then?'

'Oh, no, it was one of his companies.'

'D'you know the name?'

'He's got about half a dozen. We can easily find out which it was.'

'Does he own all the shares in these companies?'

'A majority, but not in his own name of course. He has

nominees all over the place.'

'It looks as though you may have some difficulty in proving your case.'

'I don't think so, but he won't fight it when he sees we mean business.'

'That's what everyone says.'

'Maybe, but he can't fight this case.'

'Why not?'

'He's a Member of Parliament, and supposed to be respectable.'

'Well, what of it?'

'I happen to know something about Mr Gloster which the public doesn't – yet.'

'Oh?'

'He once served a sentence of a year's imprisonment for fraud in the USA.'

'How d'you know?'

'I've checked up on it. Look at this.' Martin handed Mr Spratt the letter he had received from America.

'Yes, that looks all right. Quite useful. Of course, it doesn't prove our claim, but it's quite a useful little weapon. What rate of commission d'you claim?'

'Twenty per cent.'

'What on – the profit?'

'Yes.'

'How much was it?'

'No idea, but it must have run into five or six figures, at least.'

'Well, let me have the details, and we'll write to Mr Gloster and see what he says.'

A few days later Mr Gloster received the following letter.

12 Bunthorne Street,
Strand, WC2

1st July, 19 –

Braggs, Golightly and Sharpe
Solicitors
(*incorporating Hugg, Neadham
and Charlesmith*)

Harold Spratt, LLB

Dear Sir,

We have been consulted by our client, Mr Martin Painswick, in regard to a claim for commission against you, which our client informs us you are refusing to meet. Our client instructs us that on an occasion last year you asked him if he knew where you could obtain a large quantity of parachute silk and, on the terms that you would pay our client a reasonable commission on the deal, our client introduced you to a Mr Scroope. As a result of that introduction you made a very large purchase of parachute silk from the Ministry of Supply and our client requires payment of his commission on the profit you have made. Our client says that 25 per cent is the proper commission but he is prepared to accept 20 per cent if his claim is now met without delay. We shall be glad to hear that you are prepared to let us know the total profit made by you and to accord to our client his share, or alternatively we desire to have the name and address of solicitors who will accept service of a writ on your behalf. We should add that the reason for the delay in putting forward our client's claim is that he has been extremely busy with other matters, some of them involving correspond-ence with the USA.

Yours faithfully,
BRAGGS, GOLIGHTLY AND SHARPE.

A few days later they received a reply from Mr Gloster's solicitors.

Our client is amazed (*they wrote*) at the effrontery of your client's claim. Our client has only once met your client when a discussion took place about a possible sale to your client, by a company in which our client was interested, of some ladies' underwear. The business fell through as your client could not provide satisfactory references or pay cash. It is quite true that Mr Scroope did effect an introduction which resulted in the purchase to which you presumably refer. It is also true that our client made a substantial profit on the transaction. It is, however, quite untrue, as your client well knows, that your client ever introduced Mr Scroope to our client. Unfortunately (as your client presumably knows) Mr Scroope is dead, but our client is not going to let this fact deter him from contesting a bogus claim. In this connection we should like to know the meaning of the last sentence in your letter.

Almost by return of post Mr Gloster's solicitors received a reply from Messrs Braggs, Golightly and Sharpe. It ran:

It does not surprise us, in view of information which we have about your client, that your client should repudiate his obligations and instruct you to write a libellous letter to us. It does, however, surprise us that a firm of solicitors of your standing, or, indeed, any firm of solicitors, should make such allegations

114

without first enquiring into the facts. The expression 'bogus claim' is gravely defamatory of our client and unless we have an immediate withdrawal and apology from you and an offer to compensate our client in damages (a moderate sum will suffice at the present time) proceedings for libel will be taken against your firm personally. Our regret at having to take action against brother solicitors is modified by our feeling that people who write letters of that kind should be taught a lesson. We should add for your assistance that on the occasion when our client introduced your client to the late Mr Scroope (our client regrets very much to learn of his death as he would certainly have confirmed our client's statement) a witness was present who is still alive and well. You do not state that you will accept service on behalf of your client and accordingly, we have arranged for the writ to be served on him personally.

A writ for libel will be issued against your firm personally in default of the conditions referred to above being complied with in seven days.

With regard to the last sentence in your letter, the last sentence in our previous letter meant exactly what it said, ie: (i) our client had been busy, and (2) he had been corresponding with the USA.

The reply from Mr Gloster's solicitors came within a very few days:

We have not the slightest intention (*they wrote*) of apologising to your client, and we shall be obliged if you will refrain from referring to us as 'brother solicitors.' Your letter under reply imputes that we have been guilty of unprofessional conduct and, unless we receive an unqualified withdrawal and apology (we do not at the moment require damages), we shall take proceedings against your firm personally for libel. May we add that we shall have no regret whatever in taking such proceedings, which may perhaps lead you to be more careful in the future, in criticising the conduct of the solicitors on the other side just because their instructions do not coincide with yours. Our statement that your client was making a bogus claim was made by us in good faith and without malice towards your client (of whom we had never heard before) upon our client's instructions, and upon those instructions we repeat it. Our client would be very interested to know the name of the witness to an interview which did not take place. If we do not receive your apology within seven days a writ will be issued. Will you accept service yourselves?

With regard to the last sentence of your letter, we should like to know the relevance of your client's correspondence with the USA. If irrelevant, as it appears to be, it has a menacing flavour.

The reply (which was delivered by hand) was as follows:

The bearer will serve you with the writ which we warned you would be served against your firm personally. As the matters in dispute between us are going to be litigated there seems little point in continuing this correspondence, but we must deal with certain points.

We have nothing to apologise for in any of our letters. We said we were surprised at your behaviour. We were, but we shall not be in the future. We will accept service of your threatened proceedings which we can only assume are a counterblast to our client's genuine claims against you and your client.

The last sentence in your letter is extremely libellous. The plain suggestion is that this is a blackmailing claim by our client. Further proceedings will be taken in respect of this libel unless an immediate apology with substantial compensation is offered. We daresay your client would like to know the name of the witness to the interview at which your client was introduced to Mr Scroope by our client. May we respectfully suggest that you and your client should do your fishing elsewhere, though you are not likely to catch much if you bluster and make as much noise as you do in your letters.

The reply:

Having regard to your other conduct we are not surprised at your discourtesy in serving the writ upon us personally. Your letter under reply is a further libel upon us, and, in view of the previous libel and the tone of your letters, we do not propose to correspond further in the matter. The Court will be left to judge of your behaviour.

We do not propose to follow your discourteous example and accordingly we enclose two original and copy writs against your firm for acceptance of service. Please endorse the originals and return them.

We need only add that never in the course of our professional experience (and we have had to deal at times with some extremely unpleasant firms) have we been treated with such unwarranted and deliberate rudeness and discourtesy.

To which the answer (also sent by hand) was:

> We accept service of the writs issued by you and enclose original writs duly endorsed. You never informed us that you would accept service on your own behalf nor do you even now. We have accordingly not been guilty of the least discourtesy towards you. On the contrary your failure to offer to accept service (which was obviously deliberate and implied that we did not really intend to take proceedings) was most discourteous to us. As you still do not offer to accept service the bearer will serve you with a further writ and your client will again be served personally, and we should add that the same course will be taken in regard to the service of any future proceedings which your conduct may render necessary unless and until you extend to us the normal courtesies of the profession and tell us that you will accept service in the normal way.

The matter then passed out of the realm of correspondence into that of litigation, but it must not be thought that there was not ample opportunity during the course of the litigation for the respective solicitors to fire letters at each other, always, of course, at the clients' expense. Ample opportunity there was, too, for the representatives of the two firms to meet and say rude things to and about each other, again at their clients' expense. The first step to be taken after a writ has been served is for the defendant (or, if he is represented, his solicitor on his behalf) to enter an appearance to the writ. This is a purely formal proceeding. You simply go to the offices at the Law Courts or to a district registry (if the writ has been issued in the country) and fill in a form saying that an appearance has been entered and give notice of such appearance to the other side. There is, however, a limited time for taking this step – namely, eight days from the day on which the writ is served. If no appearance is entered within the required period, it is open for the plaintiff or his solicitor to take judgment in default of appearance. In that event, if his claim is for a specific sum of money, he gets judgment for that amount; if it is for damages, he gets judgment for damages to be assessed. At any time, however, before he has taken judgment it is open to the defendant, however much out of time he may be, to enter an appearance. In the present case Mr Gloster's solicitors, Messrs Toothcombe and Witley, by an unfortunate oversight, miscounted the days. Messrs Braggs, Golightly and Sharpe, wild with glee, rushed off to the Law Courts and signed judgment in default in respect of three writs, two of them for libel against Messrs Toothcombe and Witley and their client (who as principal could be held responsible for his agents' letters), and one against Mr Gloster for Martin's commission. As the clerk (a Mr Bole) was coming out from taking judgment, he ran into the clerk from Toothcombe and Witley (a Mr Drive), who was about to enter an appearance in all three actions. They knew each other by sight.

'Just signed judgment against you,' said Bole.

'What are you talking about?' asked Drive. 'Today's my last day.'

'Have another think,' said Bole.

It was a nasty shock for Mr Drive, whose responsibility it had been to enter an appearance on the last day. He knew that Bole would not have been able to sign judgment in the normal way, unless he was right. He went suddenly white, Bole *was* right. He could imagine what Mr Toothcombe would say to him.

'Look here, old boy,' he said, as coaxingly as possible, 'I must have miscounted. Let's go to the master and have it set aside by consent. I'll pay your costs. Much better than making a song and dance about it.'

'I bet you think so,' said Bole.

The position was this. If a plaintiff signs judgment in default of appearance, it is always open for the defendant to apply to the Court to have the judgment set aside and, provided he applies soon enough, can show that he has some sort of defence and will pay the costs thrown away, his application will be granted almost automatically. The application is made by a summons which is heard by a kind of minor judge called a master. By consent it would have been possible for both clerks to go to one of the masters there and then and have this done, but only by consent.

'Look here, old boy, you know it was only a slip. I'd do the same for you any day.'

'You won't have to, old man. I can count.'

'Oh, you never make mistakes, I suppose.'

'Not this time, old boy. So long.'

With a heavy heart Mr Drive went to the department just to make certain that he hadn't been bluffed. But he didn't expect any luck, and he didn't have any. Judgment had been duly signed. He went back to his office to report to his principal – Mr Toothcombe. Mr Toothcombe danced up and down like a scalded cat. Letting Braggs and Co. have the laugh on him almost before the action had begun. The anger with which he had written the letters to that firm was nothing to the display he provided for the benefit of Mr Drive. When he had finished he told Mr Drive to issue a summons to have the judgment set aside.

On being served with the summons, Mr Spratt decided to take a small risk – solely for the purpose of annoying Messrs Toothcombe and Witley. It need hardly be added that the risk was entirely at the expense of Martin. He decided to brief counsel to oppose the application to set aside the judgment. He knew that the application would be granted, but it was in the master's discretion to allow the fee for counsel attending or not as he thought fit. If he allowed it and ordered the defendant to pay the costs, the amount he would have to pay would be very much higher, and whether or not Toothcombe and Witley paid it themselves (they were certainly liable to do so, as it was entirely their fault – but he knew what he would have done) they would be extremely annoyed. A summons attended by counsel will ordinarily cost altogether not less than about £10. So Mr Spratt went down to the Temple to have a conference with Mr Kendall Grimes, a junior of long standing whom he briefed regularly. When he arrived for his appointment he found the clerk was out. 'He'll be back in a minute,' said the junior clerk – knowing quite well that it was most unlikely that he would be back in a minute, unless they didn't have a third round. His senior was making what he used to term 'a routine call.' It certainly was part of his normal routine. He was at the Feathers. The reason why Mr Spratt so much wanted to see the clerk was to impress on him the necessity for Mr Grimes attending the summons in person. One might have thought that, if Mr Grimes accepted a brief to appear on a particular matter, he would be there. But it doesn't necessarily follow. He may be engaged somewhere else and send a deputy. That is the way to give experience to younger barristers and to annoy solicitors. It cannot always be avoided, and though it is good experience for the deputy, it is sometimes rather nerve shattering for him, if he is young and has not been long in practice. For example: 'Go on,' says a hoarse voice in his ear, that of the solicitor's managing clerk, 'ask him if he's ever been bankrupt.'

'But,' whispers counsel, 'are you sure – '

'Go on,' says the voice, 'ask him.'

'Have you ever been bankrupt?'

'Certainly not! What a monstrous suggestion.'

'Mr Green,' says the judge, 'I suppose you asked that question on instructions?'

'Yes, your Honour,' says counsel, rather unhappily.

'It is a very serious allegation to make. The matter can be proved beyond doubt, and I cannot believe that the witness would dare to deny it if it were true.'

During this speech counsel is endeavouring to turn round and ask the managing clerk what to say.

'Mr Green,' goes on the judge, 'I wish you would listen to me instead of trying to take instructions from what I suspect is a very ill-informed source.'

'I'm sorry, your Honour.'

'Now, do you accept the witness's denial or do you wish for an adjournment to enable you to put the date and place of the receiving order in bankruptcy to him?'

'I accept the denial, your Honour.'

'You accept it very readily, Mr Green. I cannot believe that counsel – on the propriety of whose questions I normally rely with complete confidence – I cannot believe that counsel would put such a question without there being some justification for it. You do definitely accept it, do you?'

'Well, your Honour, perhaps I had better ask for an adjournment.'

'Well, which is it? First you ask a very grave question of the witness, then you say you accept his answer, then you say you want an adjournment; really, Mr Green, there must be some limit to all this. If you don't know what you want, I don't see how I can.'

'Will your Honour let me take instructions?'

'Well, Mr Green, if you think they can be of any assistance to you or to me, by all means do so. But, if I were you, I should think a little before you act on them.'

'Your Honour,' says the now miserable Mr Green, 'I think I ought to explain that I'm only doing this case for Mr Brown. I only saw the papers this morning.'

'Is that a reason for asking improper questions?'

'No, your Honour.'

'Then I do not see the point of the observation.'

Mr Green then turns round to the managing clerk and asks him whether to apply for an adjournment.

'You're doing this case, not me,' says the managing clerk, 'and a nice mess you're making of it. I don't care what you do. You can jump out of the window if you like.'

Mr Green starts to turn round to face the judge again, feeling very much like a small boy at school who is homesick. 'And take the judge with you,' adds the managing clerk as Mr Green turns away from him.

'Well, Mr Green, have you your instructions now? You know, I've other cases to try. It doesn't matter to me in the least how much time you waste, but I'm thinking of those concerned in the cases which come after you.'

Mr Green now devoutly wishes that he had never come to the Bar.

'Your Honour,' he begins shakily, having very little idea of what he is going to say. He pauses so long that the judge says: 'Yes, Mr Green?' in an unpleasantly encouraging tone.

'Your Honour,' begins Mr Green again.

'Yes, you said that before,' says the judge. 'It doesn't carry me very far.'

If only I'd gone into the Canadian Mounted Police, thinks Mr Green, or become a commercial traveller or anything rather than this. I don't know what to say to him. Whatever I say will be wrong. I should like to drop my papers and run away. At that moment the managing clerk puts in a word: 'Go on, say something.'

Something moves inside Mr Green. He turns round to the managing clerk, 'Shut up!' he says. In those two words he has made an enemy for life. The managing clerk is outraged at a twopennyhalfpenny whipper-snapper talking to him like that. He makes a mental note never in any circumstances to brief Mr Green. However, Mr Green isn't at the moment worrying about his future; he's only concerned (and very much concerned) with his present. Eventually he manages to find something to say and after a five-minute lecture by the judge and a further ten minutes of agony while he loses the case, he retires to the robing-room, very red and very hot.

The managing clerk simply says: 'I'll take the papers,' and goes away.

Mr Green goes sorrowfully back to chambers, trying, not very successfully, to convince himself that there was nothing else he could have done in the circumstances. He meets Mr Brown as he gets into chambers.

'Win that all right?' says Mr Brown.

On being told the result: 'Oh, well, it can't be helped. Thanks very much. I expect you did everything possible.' By this Mr Brown means that it could have been helped.

Subsequently they have a post-mortem and Mr Green has to endure things like this:

'What did he say when you asked him about the cheque?'

'As a matter of fact, I don't think I did ask him about it.'

'Not ask him about the cheque? Oh – well, never mind. Anyway, how did the judge get over *Abbot and Crankshaft*?'

'Well – I didn't actually read it to him – '

'Not read it to him?'

'He said he knew all about it.'

'And you left it at that?'

'I'm afraid so.'

'Oh – well, never mind. I expect you put up a jolly good show really.'

Well, Mr Green could have learned a great deal from his experience. His future partly depends on how much he really did learn. Most practitioners (however brilliant their later career) have been a Mr Green in their time. It isn't, therefore, so bad for them, but the litigants who provide them with the experience don't fare quite so well. That was the sort of thing which Mr Spratt wished to avoid.

Before the clerk had returned, he went into Mr Grimes' room. It was traditionally dirty, Mr Grimes having been in practice too long to be infected with the new-fangled idea, which is slowly spreading in the Temple, that there is no real objection to a clean, orderly, well-furnished set of chambers with a decent lavatory.

'How are you, my dear fellow?' said Mr Grimes cordially. He was always very cordial to his clients. 'Very glad to see you. Now, what can I do for Mr Spratt? Take a chair, my dear fellow. That's right, that's right, that's right.'

He had a little habit of repeating his last words two or three times.

'It's only a small thing really, Mr Grimes, but I feel rather strongly about it.'

He then explained what the position was.

'I'd like you to see the correspondence, Mr Grimes.' It is an extraordinary thing that solicitors are always most proud of the letters of which they should be most ashamed.

'They're dreadful people, Toothcombe and Witley,' he added.

Mr Grimes read the correspondence. To himself he said what any intelligent person would have said and, for all his mannerisms, Mr Grimes was quite intelligent. To Mr Spratt he said: 'Well, we'll do the best we can for you, my dear fellow, but the masters are very difficult about these things. They were only a day late, and you didn't actually give them any warning.'

'Why should we?' said Mr Spratt indignantly, 'after the way they behaved.'

'Quite, my dear fellow, but the masters are so difficult, so difficult, so difficult.'

'Well, Mr Grimes, if you don't think there's any point in my briefing you,' began Mr Spratt.

'It's a toss up, my dear fellow. You never know, we can have a try. That's the way.'

'All right, Mr Grimes, if you think there's a fair chance of getting the costs and a certificate for counsel, I'll put it in Counsel's list.'

'There's a chance, my dear fellow, but I can't say more than that – can't say more than that.'

'All right, we'll chance it. Thank you very much, Mr Grimes. You will be there yourself, won't you? I haven't yet been able to see your clerk.'

'Oh, yes, I'll be there, my dear fellow, I'll be there. What would Mr Spratt think of me if I wasn't there? Goodbye, my dear fellow, goodbye, bye, bye, bye.'

Mr Spratt felt he could still hear Mr Grimes saying 'bye, bye, bye' as he reached the Strand. There he met Mr Grimes' clerk on his cheerful way back to chambers.

'How are you, Mr Spratt? Just been to see us, have you?'

'Yes, a summons for Monday. You can be there, can't you?'

'Sir, sir, sir; have we ever let you down before?'

'Well, not often,' conceded Mr Spratt.

'When, sir, never sir, we shall be there, sir,' and happily, uncertainly, but (in his own mind) efficiently, Mr Grimes' clerk rolled away.

CHAPTER TWELVE

Master in Chambers

Summonses are heard in private in a room in which the master sits behind a counter, and counsel or solicitor or solicitor's clerks or litigants in person, as the case may be, address him from in front of the counter. Large numbers of summonses are issued, and many of them are quite unnecessary. A summons has to be issued whenever one side wants something which the other side will not give. This may apply to many things during the course of one action. A summons may relate to particulars which the plaintiff wants of the defendant's defence, to a document which the plaintiff refuses to let the defendant see, to inspection of the defendant's factory, or to a host of other things. In many cases either the person asking has no right to the thing for which he is asking, or the person asked ought to have conceded the point without a summons being issued. Some people seem to think that the reason why the leading barristers win nearly all their summonses is because of the weight which their experience, reputation and ability has with the masters. This is so only to a very limited extent indeed. The real reason why they win is because in the normal way they never let their clients oppose a request which ought to be granted, or press a request which ought not to be granted. There are, of course, from time to time some extremely difficult matters which have to be fought out on a summons and may affect seriously the whole litigation. Sometimes, too, the result of a summons is vital to one party or the other. But these cases are the exception. There are also some routine summonses which have to be taken out in any event. The amount of money wasted, however, owing to the ignorance and obstinacy of some counsel and solicitors is substantial. Some of them seem to think that a sufficient reason for refusing a request by the other side is the fact that it has been made. In the present case, for example, in the first place Messrs Braggs and Co. should not have signed judgment without writing a letter warning the defendant's solicitors that, if they did not enter an appearance at once, judgment would be signed. They knew quite well that a mistake must have been made and that the defendants did not intend to let the actions go by default. Secondly, having signed judgment, Mr Bole should have agreed to Mr Drive's request to have the judgments set aside at once. The cost would have been negligible. As it was, an expenditure of about £10 was about to be incurred on a matter which could only end in one way. It can be said to the credit of solicitors and counsel that it is only in a very small percentage of cases that summonses are issued or opposed with a view to increasing the costs (though such cases do undoubtedly occur from time to time); the usual reason is obstinacy, ignorance or stupidity. These three qualities add considerably to the cost of litigation. It may be said that there has been some marked improvement during the last twenty-five years, but there is room for a good deal more. It will be appreciated that the five actions which were now pending, one as a result of Martin's claim for commission and four as a result of the acrimonious correspondence between the solicitors, gave ample scope to both sides to incur unnecessary costs, particularly as each side would now be watching the other, waiting for some mistake.

In due course the summons to set aside the judgments came on for hearing. It was last in Master Peabody's list. This meant that both counsel had to wait some time to be heard. It was open to them to agree to go before another master, if one happened to be free, but this could only be done by consent. On the day in question, when the two counsel met outside the room where the summons was to be heard, Mr Grimes said to his opponent, Mr Larkins: 'My dear fellow, would you go before another master? We'll have to wait here quite a long time.'

'It depends which,' said Mr Larkins. 'I won't go before Trotter in any circumstances. I don't mind any of the others.'

Mr Larkins' judgment of Master Trotter was the generally accepted one. The masters, like the judges, vary in ability. Master Trotter came well at the bottom of the class. He was pleasant enough, except when he lost his temper – which on an average was not more than three times a day – but his mind was so small and so heavily fortified on the outside that it was almost impossible to penetrate it. In consequence, the only people who willingly went before him were those who had a bad case. You never knew what might happen.

Before Mr Grimes could reply, Mr Larkins went on: 'But won't you agree to an order? There's nothing in this. The judgment's bound to be set aside. It's only a haggle over costs. I'll agree to costs in cause.' This would have meant that the costs would follow the eventual result of the action.

'I daresay you would, my dear fellow. I daresay you would. Is there anything else you would like as well, my dear fellow?'

'All right. We'll have to fight, but it was a bit sharp of your people, and I'm going to ask for the costs.'

'We shall see, my dear fellow, we shall see. Seems a bit novel that a defendant who's out of time should ask for the costs of putting himself right, but we shall see, my dear fellow, we shall see.'

Meanwhile, Mr Spratt had arrived a little out of breath.

'Ah! I'm glad you haven't gone in yet,' he said.

'How are you, my dear fellow, how are you? We'd always wait for Mr Spratt, wouldn't we?'

'I shouldn't have wanted you to wait, but I'd like to be there.'

'You'll be there, Mr Spratt, you'll be there. We may all be here some time. The amount of time we waste standing about here is dreadful. I don't mind telling you, my dear fellow, I think it's a scandal. Always have thought so. A scandal, that's what it is, my dear fellow, a scandal.'

No other available master could be found, but at last Master Peabody had finished the other cases in his list, and Mr Grimes and Mr Larkins, followed by their respective solicitors, walked in. As Master Peabody saw Mr Grimes, an acute observer might have detected him give the suspicion of a sigh. Mr Grimes was what was known as a fighter. However bad his case, however clear the judge or master may have made it that he was going to decide against him, Mr Grimes argued and argued, repeating himself time and again; practically no one could stop him. If the tribunal said nothing, he just went on and on and on. If the tribunal interrupted, it merely added fuel to the flames of his eloquence and gave him something extra to say. Master Peabody, having finished all his cases but one, was looking forward to leaving early when he saw Mr Grimes. However, he quickly controlled his automatic reaction and sat back in his chair to await the onslaught. He was one of the best masters. In face he resembled Mr Pickwick, and he was quite as friendly. At the same time he had a judicial mind and manner, an excellent knowledge of the practice, a quiet and occasionally mischievous sense of fun, and a great fund of patience. Perhaps that was his only fault. Too much patience on these occasions is inclined to prolong the hearing, particularly in the case of advocates like Mr Grimes. The master was relieved that Mr Grimes' opponent was Mr Larkins, and not, say, 'Foaming Billy,' as Mr William Chance was commonly called. This nickname was partly due to the fact that Mr Chance was as eloquent and persistent as Mr Grimes, and partly due to the fact that his floods of oratory were literally floods – or perhaps spray is a more appropriate word. They tell a story (no doubt quite untrue) of an occasion when counsel opposed to 'Foaming Billy' on a summons before a master, held his brief up between him and 'Foaming Billy,' while the latter was speaking.

'Why are you holding your brief like that?' asked the master.

'Please, Master, he's splashing me.'

'Splashing you? Splashing you? Why – good gracious, he's been splashing me too. I couldn't make out why my glasses were getting blurred.'

Mr Larkins began to address the master.

'Master,' he said, 'this is an application to set aside judgment in default of appearance. I don't know why my learned friend Mr Grimes is here to oppose it.'

'My learned friend is here,' put in Mr Grimes.

'You put it in counsel's list,' replied Mr Larkins.

'I think I'll hear Mr Larkins first, Mr Grimes,' put in the master gently.

'If you please, Master, if you please,' said Mr Grimes.

'My clients were one day out. They miscounted the day. The clerk who signed judgment actually met my client's clerk who was going to enter an appearance. He offered to pay the costs if the plaintiff would agree to the judgment being set aside at once, but they wouldn't hear of it.'

'That was without prejudice, Master, I believe,' put in Mr Grimes. 'I object to my friend mentioning it.'

'It wasn't without prejudice,' retorted Mr Larkins, 'and I wish my friend would not keep interrupting.'

'But Master, Master,' said Mr Grimes, 'my friend oughtn't to mention it if it's without prejudice.'

'Really,' said Mr Larkins, 'this is too bad. Am I going to be allowed to open this summons or not?'

'Mr Grimes,' said the master, 'are your instructions quite definite that the conversation was without prejudice?'

'Will you excuse me a moment, Master?'

There was a whispered conversation between Mr Spratt and Mr Grimes in which Mr Spratt could just be heard to say: 'It might have been, I'm not sure.'

'I won't take the point, Master,' said Mr Grimes. 'My client isn't quite sure.'

'Very well,' said the master.

'Really,' said Mr Larkins, 'I'm amazed. I hope that *now* my learned friend will keep quiet while I address you. I really cannot stand these persistent and unwarranted interruptions.'

'They've stopped now,' said the master.

'For the moment,' said Mr Larkins.

'Now, don't provoke Mr Grimes, Mr Larkins.'

'There are three actions, Master, and there's an affidavit of merits showing that there is a defence in each of them.

There was no warning of any kind. It's about as bad an instance of a snapped judgment as I've ever known. I hope you will bring it home to these people that the Court does not encourage conduct of this kind, and I ask you to make the plaintiffs pay the costs of this application which is entirely due to their precipitate haste.'

'Well, your clients *were* out of time,' said the master.

Mr Spratt nodded his head vigorously in agreement. What a good master you are, he was trying to convey; you hit the nail on the end at once; good master, clever master, knock him for six, Master.

'But, of course,' the master added, 'it was only one day. Normally some kind of warning is given in a case where a defence is expected.'

Mr Spratt stopped nodding, and Mr Toothcombe took it up instead.

'Exactly, Master,' said Mr Larkins. 'Quite outrageous.'

Mr Toothcombe beamed.

'I wouldn't put it like that,' said the master, 'but a trifle quick on the draw, shall we say … I expect there's a little feeling in the case. Would you care for me to look at the correspondence?'

Both solicitors nodded vigorously.

'It's exhibited to the affidavit, Master,' said Mr Larkins.

The master picked up the bundle and began to read. As he read he could not repress a faint smile.

'Dear, dear,' he said. 'Quite a bit of feeling, really.'

He wanted to add – 'Reminds me of when I was a boy,' but managed to check himself.

Having finished reading the letters, the master turned to Mr Grimes with, 'Yes, Mr Grimes?'

Mr Grimes, once unleashed, set off like a greyhound. It would be impossible to repeat here the whole of his speech without inconvenience, because it took nearly an hour. But, among other things, he said this: 'Master, the first thing the defendant has to satisfy you about is that he has a defence to the action; he must show merits, Master, merits.'

'Quite so, Mr Grimes, but what about the affidavit?' said the master.

'I'm coming to that, Master, I'm coming to that. I'm going to submit to you, Master, that in two of the actions, at any rate, he shows no merits at all, none whatever.'

'Which two actions?'

'The two libel actions, Master. Now, Master, if you look at the letters in question, they're obviously defamatory – "bogus claim," "menacing flavour" … quite obviously defamatory, Master.'

'Isn't that a matter for the judge or jury at the trial, Mr Grimes?'

'Oh, yes, Master, if the action goes to trial; but my submission is that it shouldn't. If a defendant in a libel action doesn't enter an appearance – '

'One day out,' breathed Mr Larkins softly, but so that it could be heard.

'Really, Master, I would ask you to tell my friend not to make these offensive observations.'

'I expect I'm a little deaf, Mr Grimes. I didn't hear anything. Do continue with your argument. I'm most interested.'

'That's very kind of you, Master. I was about to say that, if the document is plainly defamatory, the defendant must show some sort of defence. He doesn't say he didn't write it, he doesn't say it's true, what defence is there?'

'If you ask me – ' began the master.

'Oh, I can't ask you questions, Master.'

'I'm delighted to answer them, Mr Grimes. What do you say to privilege as a defence?'

'Malice, Master, malice. Have you ever seen letters so full of malice?'

'On whose part, Mr Grimes?'

'On the defendants', Master, on the defendants'. I don't want to read all the letters to you again, Master – '

This meant that he was about to do so unless some immediate avoiding action were taken.

'I think I have them well in mind, Mr Grimes.'

'Thank you so much, Master, I'm sure you have, Master. In the light of those letters, Master, I submit that the only question to be decided is the amount of damages, and on that issue, of course, my friend can be heard.'

'Isn't malice a question for the judge or jury, Mr Grimes?'

'In the normal way, yes, Master, but if a defendant has a regular judgment against him he must show that he has some defence. In the present case he must show that he might win on the issue of malice.'

'Well, Mr Grimes, I'm sure you think he won't and your client probably thinks so even more definitely, but can I say that he has no chance whatever?'

'Well, Master, if he only has a very faint chance he ought to have entered an appearance in time.'

'Only one day late, Mr Grimes.'

'Yes, Master, but one day *late*.'

'Yes, Mr Grimes, but only *one* day. I don't think, Mr Grimes, I ought to turn him away from the judgment seat at this stage. After all, a good deal of heat does seem to have been engendered in the correspondence. I gather there are two actions against your clients by the defendants.'

'Yes, Master.'

'I suppose you have entered an appearance in time?' said the master with a twinkle.

'Oh, yes, Master.'

'Well, I think that if the parties want to have their quarrels decided in public, they'd better all be decided. I shall set aside the judgment in the libel actions. What about the other action?'

'Oh, Master, the affidavit does say that there was no agreement to pay commission, and, if you set aside the judgment in the two actions, I think I shall have to concede that that should be done in the third, but, Master – I do submit that – '

And Mr Grimes was about to start all over again about the libel actions. He would even have read the correspondence again if given the chance. But an hour of all this was enough even for the patience of Master Peabody.

'No, Mr Grimes,' he said pleasantly but firmly, 'you must appeal to the judge if you don't like my decision.'

'If you please, Master,' said Mr Grimes resignedly, 'if you please.'

'Now, what about terms?' said the master.

This was the real question the parties had come to fight about. Everybody, including Mr Grimes, knew quite well that the judgments would be set aside, but Mr Grimes argued so strenuously against this being done for two reasons: first, he hoped that by doing so he might in some way improve his case on the issue of terms; secondly, it was against his nature not to argue a point, however forlorn, and many of his clients came to him because of this.

'I ask for the usual terms, Master,' said Mr Grimes.

'What do you say they are?' said the master.

'All costs thrown away to be taxed and paid by the defendants as a condition of the judgments being set aside, Master. Would you say to be taxed as between solicitor and client, Master?'

'I haven't said anything yet, Mr Grimes,' replied the master. 'What do you say, Mr Larkins?'

'Master, I submit that my clients should have the costs. We've been here an hour fighting about nothing really, but my learned friend has opposed this application and lost. He ought to pay us for having to listen to him so long.'

'If my friend is going to be offensive – ' began Mr Grimes.

'I am sure you wouldn't follow suit, Mr Grimes,' interrupted the master.

'In any event,' went on Mr Larkins, 'all this waste of time is because the plaintiffs snapped a judgment.'

'I think on the whole,' said the master, 'that justice will be done if costs follow the result of the trial. Costs in cause.'

'But, Master,' put in Mr Grimes, 'I hadn't finished my submission on costs. I thought you were going to put the defendants on terms.'

'Costs in cause, Mr Grimes,' said the master.

'But, Master, Master,' said Mr Grimes, his voice rising as though in agony, 'I want to address you further on the matter – '

'I'm afraid you'll have to keep it for the judge, Mr Grimes,' said the master pleasantly.

'If you please, Master, if you please.'

Although Mr Grimes took a lot of stopping, once he was really stopped he deflated like a pricked balloon – though, of course, he was ready to go on on any other subject if the occasion offered.

'Will you certify for counsel, Master?' asked Mr Larkins.

'Well,' said the master, 'you have, of course, been of the greatest assistance to me, but, on the whole, I think it was a case which your solicitors could have dealt with quite competently; certainly, judging from the correspondence, there would have been no lack of advocacy. No, I'm afraid not, Mr Larkins.'

'But I was brought here, Master. The other side put it in counsel's list.'

'Very pleased to see you, Mr Larkins, but in this particular case I think the order I have made is about right. I thank you very much, both of you.'

'Too bad, my dear fellow,' said Mr Grimes, when they were outside the master's room, in an effort to comfort Mr Spratt, 'but they will do these things, you know, they will do these things.'

The net result of all this was that, whatever happened in the case, both Martin Painswick and his opponent would be about £5 out of pocket, and neither had anything to show for the money. There should be some simple means of making solicitors themselves pay for frolics of this kind, but in practice there is not.

CHAPTER THIRTEEN

Caroline in Charge

While Mr Spratt and Mr Toothcombe were making their way back to their respective offices, both of them dissatisfied with the result of the summons (as it was Master Peabody's very proper intention that they should be), enquiries, flowers, fruit, vegetables and other gifts were pouring into the vicarage at Tapworth Magna. Those from the local people were mostly prompted by the deep affection in which they held their vicar. Even Mrs Poulter, when she sent round a dozen eggs and a pot of honey, was purely altruistic in her motives and did not expect a certainty for the following week in return. But the world outside Tapworth Magna did not propose to drop the vicar just because he had had a stroke. Too bad if he didn't recover. Too bad if he made a partial recovery but insufficient to enable him to carry on with his hobby. Until there was more definite news for the worse, it was worth while keeping in touch. It would have been rather overwhelming for Caroline if she had not decided to employ a secretary to deal with the telegrams, letters and gifts. Here is one of the letters.

Dear Sir,

I do not know whether you will be in a good enough condition of health to read this, but I humbly pray that you will be. If not, perhaps your wife will do so for you and tell you the contents. Although a stranger to you I was deeply touched by the last sermon you preached before you were taken ill. The sincerity in your voice and your choice of language almost brought me to tears. Unfortunately I have lost my dear wife, and although I have tried for some years to find her (she was last heard of in Australia), I have met with no success. It is a very difficult position for me. I have met a young lady, whom, had I not met my dear wife, I should have wished to marry. I was married in a church but the young lady is very fond of me and I am very fond of the young lady. She is a respectable young lady and I am very nearly as respectable. I must confess that when I came to your church I had not anticipated asking your advice upon this matter. I came to Tapworth Magna because I had heard of your interesting hobby and I thought I would like to take it up – not, of course (I hope you will believe this), for the purpose of gain, but as I am tired of doing crossword puzzles and the young lady to whom I referred suggested it would be fun to try something else. I think gambling is a grave curse, but it must be very thrilling to be able to pick out winner after winner and watch for the result in the evening papers or listen to it on the wireless. The young lady also thinks it would be thrilling, but she would like to know how it is done and she suggested that I should ask you for a sample. For instance, what will win the St Leger, and why? So the questions I most earnestly beg of you to answer as soon as your health permits (the St Leger is still some little way off) are:

(1)What shall I do about my wife?

(2)What shall I do about the young lady?

(3)(This, of course, is the least important, and please don't bother about it if it is a trouble but it would be really rather nice to know; so do let me know if you can.) What will win the St Leger (or any other race or races you prefer to mention)?

To which the secretary replied:

Mr Meeson-Smith is unfortunately too ill to deal with correspondence at the moment. In the meantime, may I convey to you what I am sure would be his sincere sympathy on your matrimonial difficulties? As soon as he is well enough I will bring that part of your letter to his notice. I will ignore, as you suggest, the remainder of your letter.

A reply came by return:

On reflection (*it said*) I should be glad if you would bring the remainder of my letter to the attention of Mr Meeson-Smith, if possible before September (this is rather important as the St Leger is in the second week of that month). The young lady and I are praying that Mr Meeson-Smith will soon be restored to full health. I have still not heard from my wife.

The secretary replied:

You will be glad to hear that Mr Meeson-Smith is a little better. You will not be glad to hear that I also have reflected and have treated both your letters as I should have treated the first.

She really had not the time to write letters of this kind, but when she first started the job, she took a mischievous pleasure in doing so. She was dealing with a batch of them one morning when Mrs Poulter arrived. The door was open and she had just walked in.

'Oh,' said Mrs Poulter. 'Oh – I'm s-sorry. Is Mrs M-Meeson-Smith in?'

'I'm the secretary. 'What name is it, please?'

'P-Poulter. Mrs Poulter.'

'I'll tell Mrs Meeson-Smith. Is she expecting you?'

'N-no. I just came round to see if I could be of any help.'

'It's very good of you. I'll call Mrs Meeson-Smith.' The secretary went out, taking her correspondence with her, and shortly afterwards Caroline came in.

'How very kind of you,' she said.

'How is the vicar?'

'I'm pleased to say that he is improving steadily, but it's bound to be a slow business.'

'Oh, I'm so glad he's getting on. It must be terribly worrying for you – and such an expense with secretaries and things.'

'I found I couldn't cope without. It's rather extravagant, I'm afraid. Talking of which, there is something you could do for me, if you happen to be going to Poppleton.'

'Of course I'll go. Only too delighted.'

'I want to find out about getting water and electricity laid on to the vicarage. You know, licences and things. I don't quite know where to begin. I'd get Miss Brinton to go, but she has so many letters to deal with.'

'Wh-W-Why, yes, of course I'll enquire, but I am afraid it will c-c-cost rather a lot.'

'I thought I might as well do it properly while I was about it.'

'I know it's very imp-p-pertinent of me, but you haven't been b-b-backing horses by any chance?'

'Mrs Poulter, I'm surprised at you. I had a letter the other day. I'll show it you.' She got out the letter she had shown to the Bishop and handed it to Mrs Poulter.

'G-good gracious! What a p-piece of luck! Of c-course I won't tell a soul. I'll treat it as quite c-confidential.'

'But don't, Mrs Poulter. I'm quite happy for everyone to know of our good fortune. There is no secret about it.'

She didn't add that she wouldn't have told Mrs Poulter if there had been, nor that her reason for showing the letter was in order that the news might be spread as widely as possible. She had already chatted about the letter on the telephone so as to have the benefit of Mrs Pace's publicity service.

'I wonder who the p-person was. It wasn't me, I'm afraid, though if only your husband had given me a few tips now and again it might well have been.'

'The person in question said that he wished to remain anonymous. I think it would be very ungrateful of us if in those circumstances we tried to find out who it was.'

'I suppose I mustn't ask – '

'£15,000,' said the vicar's wife. 'You can tell anyone like.'

'£15,000!' echoed Mrs Poulter. 'That's a lot of m-money. When your husband recovers you could easily turn that into £150,000, you know.'

'Mrs Poulter, you know the vicar's views on these matters, and anyway £15,000 is quite enough for anyone.'

'I don't see why you shouldn't let someone else turn it into £150,000. If you don't want the extra, I know p-plenty of p-people who do – one especially. But it's no good, I suppose. You always do what your husband says; I never did.'

'Wellsby would be most unhappy if he thought that we owed our position to betting. He would never be a party to anything of that kind. Naturally I must have regard to his views. Now, if you really can help me by enquiring about licences and so forth, I'd be most awfully grateful.'

Mrs Poulter did what she was asked, and the final consequence of these first enquiries, and of Caroline's interview with the Bishop, was that by the time the vicar was on his feet again, the vicarage was his, there was electric light, and no special precautions had to be taken about water in the dry season. It had, like everything else, been laid on by Caroline.

CHAPTER FOURTEEN

Interlocutory Proceedings

Martin's action (together with the satellite actions of the solicitors themselves) went ahead quite quickly. His was a very simple case. Too simple, really, though it was safer than 'kite flying,' and had a fair chance of success. The recipe runs something like this.

You find a wealthy businessman with a moderately unsavoury past. That is not terribly difficult. If he happens to be a Member of Parliament or a mayor or filling some other public position, so much the better. You wait until he has brought off some perfectly legitimate deal. There is no trouble about that. You then say that you introduced the deal to him directly or indirectly on the terms that you would be paid commission. There are various ways of proving your introduction, but the one which is most satisfactory, can be used if a man, who really was a link in the chain of introduction, is dead. You then claim that you introduced the wealthy businessman to the dead man. Only your opponent can dispute that you did, but you have available as a witness your partner in crime, although he professes to have no interest whatever in your claim. Now what is the position? Here are you, a person against whom (at the moment) nothing discreditable is known, and your partner, a person in a similar position, both swearing that a certain interview has taken place and there is only the defendant to deny it. But when he does deny it, you are able to discredit his evidence somewhat by bringing up his unsavoury past. In the case of Mr Gloster, it was the conviction for fraud in America. You may think that most people would have known about such a conviction, but this is by no means always the case. Even the police did not know it. Both Mr Merryweather and Mr Huntley had felt instinctively that there was something wrong with the claim and hence they would have nothing to do with it. On the face of it, there was nothing wrong whatsoever. It was just a little too simple, and, although likely to succeed, liable to be destroyed by something equally simple. When you try to prove that something has happened which has never happened at all, it is astounding how often the nakedness of the land suddenly appears. The mistake that most people make is failing to clothe their dummy with the clothes it would have been likely to be wearing had it been genuine. When a real interview of this kind takes place, all sorts of things are said, but it is surprising how often it is that, when the interview is a pure fake, the only thing which the perjurer can remember about it is the one sentence which suits his purpose. In consequence, there is no life to his story, and, fortunately, it is often (and indeed usually) disbelieved. It is not easy to invent interviews with success. The only thing of that kind which is more difficult is forgery. That is an extremely difficult task and very rarely succeeds. There are so many pitfalls that it is most probable that the forger will fall into one of them at some stage of the proceedings. In the present case Martin took no such chances. He did not suggest that there was anything in writing. His case was that he trusted Mr Gloster who, after all, was a Member of Parliament. Not infrequently

147

commission agreements of the kind may be made by word of mouth, and, by carelessness, each side may forget or not bother to confirm in writing. Martin also had in mind that, from Mr Gloster's point of view, there was not only the possibility of his losing the action but there was the possibility that his conviction in the USA would be made public. Although Mr Gloster did not tell his solicitors immediately what the reference to the USA in the first letter must certainly have been, he realised that he was being blackmailed. It was a very serious matter for him. It was the most deadly form of blackmail because it could not be stigmatised as such in its initial stages. There could be no 'Mr X' for Mr Gloster.

'Make sure you tell him,' said Martin to Mr Spratt, 'that I've been in correspondence with the USA.'

Mr Spratt was prepared to do what he was asked to do, though a more reputable solicitor would, of course, have refused.

Martin prepared his case very thoroughly. He worked out the interview carefully with Mr Fuller, giving it real flesh and blood, and ensuring that his story and Mr Fuller's should not be exactly the same except on essential matters. Although, however, his claim against Mr Gloster was contained in formal legal documents and made through the Courts, had the truth of the matter been proved he could have been convicted of blackmail just as if his demand had been barefaced and by letter signed 'The Black Hand.' It is as well that people, who bring proceedings for which they know there is no foundation, should realise this. Blackmail is a dreadful crime, and Martin had only two excuses for committing it – first, he needed the money; secondly, Mr Gloster was, in effect, an impostor and ought not to have been allowed to remain a Member of Parliament. He was quite as crooked as Martin.

But, of course, that is the sort of person whom it is easy to blackmail. It is next to the impossible to obtain anything by threats from a person who has nothing to fear. Martin was certainly reverting to type. Although old Uriah Painswick settled down to an otherwise respectable life after retiring from 'the road' to become an innkeeper, he could not resist supplementing his income by extracting levies from highwaymen in return for his silence. If they paid, however, he did not inform against them thereafter, unless it was absolutely necessary for his own preservation. Strange that none of Uriah's vices were to be found in Mr Justice Painswick, and yet most of them in his son. This was certainly not due to the judge's late wife, who was herself a person of the highest character and who came from a long line of virtuous parents.

Although, as has already appeared in the case of Mr and Mrs Trent, the law can act with extreme rapidity when necessary, a civil action normally proceeds at only a moderate pace and may be a long time before it is heard. This would not have suited Martin, who was staving off his creditors with some of the money furnished by his father and with promises of the fruits of this action against Mr Gloster. Accordingly, he instructed Mr Spratt to set a fast pace. In the course of an action, each side has to deliver a number of documents to the other, and there is a time limit for such delivery. If a party cannot deliver the document within the time limited, he applies to his opponent for an extension of time. This is usually, though not always, granted in the first instance, but if it is refused or if a later request is refused, a summons for an extension of time has to be issued. Solicitors sometimes get quite angry with their opponents on the subject of extension of time, and allegations of trying to delay the action are frequent in their correspondence on this matter. One such dispute resulted in what must be the shortest letter on record. It is an old story, but it has the merit of truth, and as it has never been told in writing before, here it is. It consists of two letters, the first from Solicitor A to solicitor B, and the second from B to A.

Dear Sirs,

We have received your letter of the 20th ult. We think we had better set the facts on record. On the 1st May your defence became due and you asked for an extension of fourteen days, which we granted. On the 5th May, after we warned you on the telephone that, as no defence has been delivered, we should sign judgment in default, you asked us for a further ten days, and this was granted. On the day before the defence was due, you asked for a further extension of seven days. When we refused you issued a summons and were granted a further seven days. The defence not being delivered within that time, we again telephoned you out of courtesy to warn you, and you asked for a further three days, promising that the defence would be duly delivered within that time. I've acceded to your request. Are we now to understand that you are asking us to give you yet a further seven days' extension?

Yours faithfully,

A.

Back came the reply:

Dear Sirs,
Yes.
Yours faithfully,

B.

In *Painswick v Gloster and Others*, no extensions of time were granted by either side, and so, whenever extra time was wanted, a summons was issued and the application for time bitterly opposed. In addition to such summonses, several others were issued in the course of the litigation. Among them was one issued by the defendant to ascertain certain particulars of Martin's Statement of Claim. A Statement of Claim is a document which sets out in detail the demands of the plaintiff. The most important item from Mr Gloster's point of view was the place and date of the interview when the alleged agreement was supposed to have been made. This had been left fairly vague in the Statement of Claim. As the result of an order for particulars, however, Martin was pinned down to a 'date in May which the plaintiff cannot more particularly specify at the Cleveland Palace Hotel at about 12.30 p.m.' The defendant had sought unsuccessfully to obtain the name of the alleged witness. A party is not entitled to be told the names of the other side's witnesses, but he may learn them incidentally if he can show that mention of the names is necessary to a clear presentation of the other party's case. That was the ground on which this information was asked for in Martin's case.

'The plaintiff has not said on which date the interview was, but only that it was in May. How can the defendant identify it on that information?'

The master pointed out that the defendant said there was no interview with the plaintiff at all at that time. How could it legitimately help him to be told the name of the witness?

'No order,' said the master.

Another dispute, however, assumed much larger proportions and actually went to the Court of Appeal. The beginning of Martin's Statement of Claim was as follows:

The Defendant Gloster is and was at all material times a Member of Parliament. The Defendant firm acts and at all material times acted as his solicitors and in particular wrote the letters complained of in paragraph 5 hereof on the instructions of and on behalf of the Defendant Gloster.

The document then went on to allege the agreement to pay commission and the failure to pay it and then to complain of the allegedly libellous letters.

The defendants applied to have the first sentence of the first paragraph of the Statement of Claim struck out as being scandalous or unnecessary or as an abuse of the process of the Court or likely to prejudice the fair trial of the action.

Master Trotter struck out the allegation.

The plaintiff appealed to the Judge in Chambers, who restored it, and the defendant obtained leave from the judge (who had only recently been appointed) to appeal to the Court of Appeal.

(The total costs involved in summonses and appeals of this kind may approach £100, and no one is normally any better off [apart from the counsel and solicitors involved] except that, if one side obtains all the costs against the other, the payment of such a bill before an action comes on for trial can act as a discouragement to the party who has to pay. Sometimes, therefore, such applications are indulged in by counsel solely for this purpose.)

The defendants argued that the fact that Mr Gloster was a Member of Parliament was wholly irrelevant to the proceedings and had only been inserted as an implied threat to Mr Gloster, the threat being that of publicity. The plaintiff disclaimed any such object.

'If,' said Mr Grimes, 'the action had only been for commission, the allegations would certainly have been irrelevant and would not have been made. There are, however, claims for libel as well. The character of the libeller must be relevant. A libel by a notorious criminal carries little weight. One by a Church dignitary or a Member of Parliament is of far greater importance and may add to the damages.'

To this Mr Spelthorne, KC (leading Mr Larkins) replied that, if the libel had been in a newspaper or book or in a letter to a stranger, that might have been the case. In fact, however, the publication of the libel was a pure technicality, being only to the typists or clerks or partners in the two firms of solicitors. He repeated that the only object of the sentence was to try to frighten Mr Gloster.

'Well,' put in Lord Justice Mew, after Mr Spelthorne had gone on in reply for some time, 'you are responsible for the publicity so far. No one would have known anything about it if you hadn't appealed from the Judge in Chambers.'

'That may be, my Lord, but – '

'Surely,' said Lord Justice Rowe, 'this was a matter for the discretion of the learned Judge in Chambers? How can we interfere with his discretion?'

'My Lord, I respectfully submit that – '

'Really, Mr Spelthorne,' said Lord Justice Mew, 'I cannot think how your client is in the least prejudiced. Granted that the allegation may not affect the damages very acutely, what harm does it do?'

'I respectfully suggest, my Lord – '

'You haven't yet answered the criticism that it is you who are causing all the publicity at the moment,' added Lord Justice Torr.

'My Lord, that criticism – '

'I notice,' said Lord Justice Rowe, 'that the name of the plaintiff is a very distinguished legal name. That hasn't by any chance anything to do with the publicity now being accorded to the case?'

'My Lord, I am sorry to think – '

'Really, Mr Spelthorne,' said Lord Justice Mew, 'can you carry the matter any further? We've already heard you at some length.'

'I would like to say this,' said Mr Spelthorne, 'the publicity in your Lordships' Court – '

'But that has really nothing to do with the matter,' put in Lord Justice Torr. 'It was only mentioned in passing by my brother when you were complaining of threats. I think you've said everything that can possibly be said, Mr Spelthorne.'

'Rather more,' whispered Lord Justice Mew, in an aside to Lord Justice Rowe.

So Mr Spelthorne sat down, the appeal was dismissed with costs, and Mr Spratt walked out of the Court, his face wreathed in smiles.

'Better luck next time,' he said, with an exasperating grin, to Mr Toothcombe.

Mr Toothcombe made no reply, but turned his back on him and spoke to Mr Spelthorne.

'One can't always be up against gentlemen,' he said.

'Did you say something?' asked Mr Spratt angrily.

'Yes,' said Mr Toothcombe, 'to Mr Spelthorne.'

'Well, I should be a little careful if I were you,' said Mr Spratt.

Mr Toothcombe again turned his back on Mr Spratt and addressed Mr Spelthorne. 'Listeners,' he said, 'seldom hear any good of themselves.'

It is extraordinary how many grown-up people behave at times as though they were still in the Lower Fourth. This is by no means confined to solicitors.

Eventually the time arrived for what is called discovery of documents. Each party has to disclose in an affidavit all the documents which are, or ever have been, in his possession, custody or power. The affidavit is prepared by the solicitor and sworn by the client. Such affidavits are notoriously incomplete. This is sometimes due to a client not making sufficient disclosure to his solicitor, sometimes to a solicitor not asking sufficient questions of his client, and, more often than not, to the affidavit being carelessly prepared in the solicitor's office. The arrival of the time for discovery presented an acute problem to Mr Toothcombe. If he had been a solicitor of integrity, it would have presented no problem at all. He was not a man who would have dreamed of converting his clients' money, or doing anything of that nature. But, when it came to discovery of documents, he was quite prepared to stretch a point (as he called drawing up a false affidavit). He was particularly prepared to do so in the present case where he was determined to hit the plaintiff, and his solicitors, as hard as possible. He was, in fact, in a very strong position to do this. It has already been pointed out that a simple case, based on faked evidence, may sometimes be destroyed very simply. The document about which Mr Toothcombe could not make up his mind was Mr Gloster's passport, which showed that he was out of England from April 3rd to July 1st. If that document were to be disclosed in his client's affidavit (as, of course, it should have been) it might have one of two results. The plaintiff might surrender at once. This would be too soon for Mr Toothcombe's liking – insufficient costs would have been incurred and it would be much more effective and pleasant to see the discomfiture of Mr Spratt in open court. The other possible result would be that the plaintiff would amend his Statement of Claim, and allege that the agreement took place in a different month. He would, of course, have to make some excuse for the mistake and this would not be easy. It would not, however, be impossible, and it might be that the plaintiff would have sufficient ingenuity to invent a plausible tale. If, however, the passport were suddenly produced in Court after the plaintiff had in cross-examination been compelled to pledge himself to the month of May, and no other month, it would then be too late. Mr Toothcombe could imagine the cross-examination:

MR SPELTHORNE, KC: Are you sure this interview took place?

THE PLAINTIFF: Of course I am.

MR SPELTHORNE, KC: And that it took place at the Cleveland Palace Hotel?

THE PLAINTIFF: Certainly.

MR SPELTHORNE, KC: And in May?

THE PLAINTIFF: Yes.

MR SPELTHORNE, KC: Why so sure it was at the Cleveland Palace Hotel?

THE PLAINTIFF: Because I remember being there. We were in the lounge. We'd just had or were about to have a drink. We certainly had one with Mr Gloster. I had a sherry – Tio Pepe – that's easy to remember because I always have one. I can't honestly remember what Mr Gloster had. It may have been a dry Martini. I'm not sure.

MR SPELTHORNE, KC: What did Mr Fuller have?

THE PLAINTIFF: I really can't remember at this distance of time. All I do know is that we had drinks, and mine was Tio Pepe.

156

MR SPELTHORNE, KC: Are you quite sure it was in May?

THE PLAINTIFF: Positive.

MR SPELTHORNE, KC: Why so sure?

THE PLAINTIFF: Because, as a matter of fact, we went to the theatre that night and I remember the play, *Bitter Almonds*.

MR SPELTHORNE, KC: But that play was on in April, June and July, was it not?

THE PLAINTIFF: As a matter of fact, it was not. It wasn't on at one of the West End theatres, but at one of the small repertory theatres. It only ran for a month, May.

MR SPELTHORNE, KC: Quite sure of that? How do you know?

THE PLAINTIFF: I've looked it up.

MR SPELTHORNE, KC: No possibility of mistake, I suppose?

THE PLAINTIFF: None whatever.

MR SPELTHORNE, KC: And so you swear beyond any question of doubt or mistake that on some date in May you met Mr Gloster in the Cleveland Palace Hotel?

THE PLAINTIFF: I've already done so.

MR SPELTHORNE, KC: And you don't want to go back on it?

THE PLAINTIFF: Certainly not.

At this stage in his imagination Mr Toothcombe positively oozed with excitement. The plaintiff had been tied up completely. There was no hope of retreat and the ripe plum, all ready for plucking, was about to be plucked. A lovely moment. There would, of course, be a bit of a song and dance about the non-disclosure of the passport, but that would be lost in the complete overthrow of the plaintiff. This is how it would go:

MR SPELTHORNE, KC: Well, Mr Painswick, would you mind having a look at this?

MR GRIMES: What document are you handing to the witness?

MR SPELTHORNE, KC: You'll see.

MR GRIMES: It looks like a passport, and no passport has been disclosed.

MR SPELTHORNE, KC: It is a passport, Mr Gloster's passport. Will you look at it, please, Mr Painswick?

MR GRIMES: My Lord, I object to this. I don't know what the effect of it is –

MR SPELTHORNE, KC: I'm sure you don't.

MR GRIMES: Will my learned friend kindly not interrupt. This passport, if relevant, ought to have been disclosed.

THE JUDGE: What do you want me to do about it? Exclude it from being given in evidence?

MR GRIMES: Well, my Lord –

THE JUDGE: You know I can't do that. Of course, if it is relevant, it ought to have been disclosed, and we shall have to see what the explanation is, but I can't keep it out. Perhaps I'd better look at it first. *(After a pause)*. Yes, this does seem to show that Mr Gloster wasn't in England between April and July, but I'm not quite sure what Mr Painswick can say about it. He says he was. Perhaps he'd better look at it. D'you see that, Mr Painswick?

THE PLAINTIFF: Which page does your Lordship mean? I only see the names of countries on this page.

THE JUDGE: Now you've lost the place. Give it back to me, usher.

MR SPELTHORNE, KC: Perhaps you'd rather not see it, Mr Painswick. Still sure you saw Mr Gloster in May?

THE PLAINTIFF: Well – I suppose I could have made a mistake.

THE JUDGE: Now look at it again. Keep the place for him, usher. It does look as though Mr Gloster couldn't have been at the Cleveland Palace Hotel in May, doesn't it? Unless, of course, this is a forgery.

THE PLAINTIFF: Yes, it does look as though he couldn't have been there. I must have been wrong.

MR SPELTHORNE, KC: What about *Bitter Almonds*? You checked that.

THE PLAINTIFF: I must have mixed it up with another play. That's where the misunderstanding must have been, but I was sure it was *Bitter Almonds*. I can't understand it.

MR SPELTHORNE, KC: Of course, if the interview never took place at all, as my client says, that explains everything, doesn't it, Mr Painswick?

THE PLAINTIFF: It did take place.

MR SPELTHORNE, KC: Let me have the passport back, please. Well, as you've made a mistake – to what would you like to amend it? You'll forgive me if I ask you for an answer before you examine the passport any more? You see, you might hit on another date when Mr Gloster was abroad. What month do you now suggest?

(*No answer.*)

What year?

(*No answer.*)

What, can't you suggest one? Are you wondering, by any chance, what other alibi Mr Gloster might prove?

(*No answer.*)

Do you think it might be awkward if you made another mistake?

(*No answer.*)

You do realise you are giving evidence on oath, don't you?

(*No answer.*)

I'm only asking you one question at a time, and I'm only going on because you don't answer any of them.

THE PLAINTIFF: My Lord, I don't feel very well –

Mr Toothcombe visualised it all. It would be just perfect.

Spratt would be there, kicking himself for not having thought of it before. But if he disclosed the passport before the trial, the plaintiff could alter his story and would be prepared for the obvious cross-examination. Unfortunately Mr Gloster had no other perfect alibis that year. So the plaintiff could say March, April or July, instead of May. It was a nasty decision to have to make. He wasn't worried about the morality of it, but of the possible consequences of non-disclosure. Normally such things get by with, at the worst, a rap over the knuckles in Court. But Spratt would be vindictive and press the matter as hard as he could. Well, Gloster and he could invent a story about his having forgotten he was abroad then, and only thinking of the matter and getting hold of his passport just before the plaintiff was cross-examined. Of course, even then it ought to have been disclosed at once. If he gave it to Spelthorne too soon, he'd tell the other side. He must wait until the plaintiff was being cross-examined and take the consequences for not telling his counsel before. If however, he were pressed on that he would have to concede that he held it back so as to take the plaintiff by surprise. Well, the proof of the pudding would have to be in the eating, but some judges could be very unpleasant about it. The matter might be reported to the Law Society. After much careful thought, Mr Toothcombe eventually decided most regretfully that he mustn't take the risk. It wasn't a very large one, but it was too definite to be taken. So, into the affidavit of documents went the passport. He tried it first in the privileged documents (that is, documents which, although disclosable in the affidavit, need not be shown to the other side), but the plaintiff issued a summons, the master ordered him to produce it and an appeal to the judge failed. He didn't feel like going to the Court of Appeal again, particularly as his claim to privilege could not possibly be justified. So the plaintiff and his solicitors saw the passport – and Martin had to think again. But, as Mr Toothcombe realised sadly, it was much more pleasant for him to have to think again well before the trial, in a solicitor's office, than to have to do so in the witness box. 'It's a shame,' he said to himself. 'The rules about discovery are ridiculous.'

CHAPTER FIFTEEN

Painswick (Junior) v Gloster (Last Round)

The disclosure of the passport was a very nasty blow for Mr Spratt. He sent for Martin at once and told him.

'Oh dear,' said Martin, 'that's awkward. I must have made a mistake.'

'And your friend Mr Fuller as well?'

'Yes, he too. We often do make mistakes, you know.'

'Mr Painswick, this is a serious matter. If the interview definitely did take place, it can't have been in May.'

'No, nor June for that matter, and there's only April 1st, and 2nd, and I don't much care for the sound of the 1st, and anyway, I ought to have remembered it if it had been on that day. What about March? That begins with an "Ma" too. Perhaps it was your mistake, and not mine, and you wrote down May instead of March. Solicitors do make mistakes like that I suppose, sometimes.'

'Mr Painswick, we did not make a mistake. You know quite well that, when the defendants asked for particulars, I pressed you for the date and you said the best you could say was May. I asked you if it might have been April or June, and you said "No." '

'March isn't April or June. I didn't say it couldn't be March.'

'Mr Painswick, if I didn't know you to be a respectable son of a distinguished father, I should have grave doubts of the honesty of your claim.'

'Oh, don't bring my father into it. He's got nothing to do with it. Come to think of it, it was March. I remember now. Of course. But I suppose Mr Gloster wasn't abroad in March as well. You had a look for that too?'

'No, as I told you, he was away that year only from April 3rd to July 1st.'

'Good. Well, that's all right, then. It was March. I'm glad that's fixed. Anything else you want? When will the trial be?'

'Mr Painswick, you don't seem to appreciate the gravity of the situation at all. It's quite true we can get leave to amend our particulars by changing from May to March, but the comment which will be made by counsel for the defence will be very strong.'

'Of course it will. That's what he's paid for.'

'And in my view very effective. I think we'd better go and see Mr Grimes and get his opinion as to whether it's worth going on with the action.'

'Worth going on? What a fuss you make about a small alteration like that. Substitute "rch" for "y". You lawyers are particular. Anyway, why can't you say it was your mistake – a silly typist or something?'

'Mr Painswick, you may or may not know that, when you gave me instructions, I wrote them down. If we wanted to prove that it was my mistake, I should have to give evidence and produce my notes.'

'Well, that's simple enough. Scrap the old notes and write some more. Surely I don't have to teach you your job.'

Mr Spratt was quite used to dealing with dishonest clients, he was even quite used to stories being changed and a nod or wink passing between him and his client during the process, but this barefaced suggestion of fraud, and the open manner in which Martin wanted him to forge his notes, was a novelty to him and quite shocking. It was against all the rules of the game.

'I can only assume you are joking, Mr Painswick, and, if I may say so, not in very good taste.'

'You're a funny fellow,' said Martin. 'I thought you were on my side. I make a perfectly sensible suggestion, and instead of thanking me for it, you go off the deep end. I thought one employed a solicitor to help, not to hinder. First of all, you or your typist, or both of you, make a most important mistake, and then, when, instead of being angry, I suggest that you should do the obvious thing and put it right, you start telling me I'm acting in bad taste. It's beyond me.'

'We did not make a mistake, and you know it.'

'Just let me think. I know – we'll ask my friend Fuller; I fancy he'll confirm that both of us told you March.'

'Mr Painswick, I regret to have to say this to a client – particularly a client with such a distinguished father – '

'I asked you before. Please leave my father out of it. He wasn't at the interview, either in March or May.'

'Nor, in my opinion, Mr Painswick, was anyone else. I regret to have to say that, in my view, you are the most unprincipled scoundrel with whom I have had the misfortune to deal.'

'And what, may I ask, is your experience in that line? How many have you met? If it's only one or two, your sweeping statement counts for nothing.'

'I am not prepared to continue this conversation. I assume you would like to consult another solicitor.'

'Certainly not. I've hired you for the journey. Never change horses in mid-stream, I say – or mules,' he added.

'Mr Painswick, I was giving you the chance of withdrawing your instructions yourself, but I must tell you quite plainly that I should not dream of continuing to act for you either in this or any other matter. I will send you my firm's bill for the work done to date, and that is the last thing I have to say. I don't propose to let even a judge's son stay here and insult me. Good morning, sir.'

'Well, well, well,' said Martin. 'I've a lot to learn yet, I see. Now what do I do?'

'Leave this office, sir, if you please.'

'Very well, Mr Spratt. Goodbye, and please remember me to Mr Braggs, Mr Golightly and Mr Sharpe, and don't forget to incorporate Mr Hugg, Mr Neadham and Mr Charlesmith when you do so.'

As soon as he had gone, Mr Spratt picked up the telephone and asked to speak to Mr Toothcombe.

'Old boy,' he said, to Mr Toothcombe's surprise, '*Painswick v Gloster and Others*. I'm not acting for the plaintiff any more. I thought I'd let you know at once.'

'That's very kind of you,' said Mr Toothcombe, adopting an equally friendly tone. 'Anything the matter?'

'Plenty. I've just slung him out of my office. I won't say more, but you may want to subpoena me to be present so that I shall be available to give evidence of the instructions given to me, if the plaintiff wants to go into all that.'

'That's very civil of you, old boy.'

'Well, I thought it was the only decent thing. We've always got on very well with you in the past.'

'Of course we have, old man. I'm glad you rang up. About those libel actions – shall we call it a day as far as our firms are concerned?'

'I was just going to say the same thing. We'll write each other a friendly note and discontinue all of them, shall we?'

165

'I'll do it today. That still leaves over Painswick's claim for libel against us.'

'I shouldn't worry about that very much. Are you doing anything for lunch?'

'Wait a moment. No, I'm free.'

'Good; come and have lunch with me at the Law Society.'

'Delighted, old boy. One o'clock?'

'OK. So long. Tell you some more then.'

Mr Toothcombe was now very pleased that he had disclosed the passport. All his anger against Mr Spratt had disappeared and he had no feelings at all about the plaintiff, who would either discontinue the action or bring it to trial. In either case he would be bound to lose, now that Mr Spratt had clearly indicated what the position was. The four stupid libel actions, which were taking up time and space in the office, were out of the way, and while he enjoyed acrimonious correspondence, he equally enjoyed restoring friendly relations with his opposite numbers. He went off to meet Mr Spratt in high spirits. They had a somewhat convivial lunch in the course of which, in the strictest confidence, they told each other a number of things about their own clients which they had learned from their respective clients also in the strictest confidence.

Meanwhile Martin had to make up his mind whether he would give in, instruct another solicitor, or conduct the case in person. As he had no other plan for making enough money to satisfy his creditors and there was no time to make one, he ruled out the first course. If he fought and lost the action, he wouldn't be worse off than if he gave it up now, and there was always the chance that he would win. He realised, however, that everything would depend upon how he and Fuller could stand cross-examination on the change of month. Having regard to his experience with Mr Spratt he decided not to employ any other solicitors in case he should wish to change his story again and they also were too squeamish to be parties to it. So he went on with the action in person. First of all, he applied for and obtained leave to amend his particulars by changing May to 'in or about March.' The defendants also amended by justifying the statement that it was a bogus claim. Until the production of the passport and its consequences, they had not thought it wise to do so, but now they felt confident. Accordingly, they put as the main defence to the claim for libel that it was true. In due course the case came up for hearing before Mr Justice Pantin.

Martin gave his evidence extremely well in the first instance. He was careful to draw the judge's attention to the amendment and to say what a shock it was to him when he saw the passport. He had been quite sure it was in May. Now he realised it could not have been. It could not have been after May for various reasons which he gave and which seemed adequate. It must have been before, in March or, at the earliest, the end of February. He gave full details of the interview, making it look as though it really had taken place. Eventually Mr Spelthorne rose to cross-examine.

'Have you a good memory?' was his first question.

MARTIN: For some things, not for dates.

SPELTHORNE, KC: You seem to have details of the interview at your fingertips.

MARTIN: Is that a question or a comment to his Lordship?

SPELTHORNE, KC: Yes, it was a question. I'm sorry you did not catch the note of interrogation. I will add 'haven't you?'

MARTIN: Yes, I have. I've thought a lot about it.

SPELTHORNE, KC: Since when?

MARTIN: Ever since Mr Gloster refused to honour his promise.

SPELTHORNE, KC: And how long ago was that?

MARTIN: About nine months or so.

SPELTHORNE, KC: So for the last nine months you have had in mind the details of this interview?

MARTIN: Yes.

SPELTHORNE, KC: Including the place?

MARTIN: Yes.

SPELTHORNE, KC: And month?

MARTIN: I made a mistake about the month. I've already said so.

SPELTHORNE, KC: At the time you made the mistake the interview was under a year old.

MARTIN: Quite right. A lot can happen in a year.

SPELTHORNE, KC: You must have known, say in January, what your movements were in the preceding February, March, April and May.

MARTIN: Generally, yes, but it's very easy to confuse a month. I had a good number of interviews with a good number of people at the time.

SPELTHORNE, KC: On what subjects?

MARTIN: On all sorts.

SPELTHORNE, KC: Such as?

MARTIN: Buying goods, selling goods.

SPELTHORNE, KC: Anything else?

MARTIN: On, all manner of things, arranging things here, settling up something there, meeting friends, discussing business deals and so on, etcetera.

SPELTHORNE, KC: Any commission agreements apart from this one?

MARTIN: Very likely.

SPELTHORNE, KC: Can you mention a single one? Please bear in mind that I shall ask for details of each transaction and request you to produce the documents.

MARTIN: A lot of my work is done without documents.

SPELTHORNE, KC: Come, Mr Painswick, are you saying that you normally enter into legitimate commission agreements and have nothing in writing – not even a cheque?

MARTIN: Possibly.

SPELTHORNE, KC: Can you mention a single one with or without documents?

MARTIN: Not at the moment. I'm not prepared for a cross-examination of all my business transactions over a year. I shall have to look it up.

SPELTHORNE, KC: Then there are documents?

MARTIN: Or think about it.

SPELTHORNE, KC: Are you prepared to swear that there was a single commission agreement except the one you allege with Mr Gloster?

MARTIN: I can't be sure.

SPELTHORNE, KC: Then there can't have been many or you would swear there was at least one?

MARTIN: Possibly not.

THE JUDGE: It does not sound as though there can have been many.

MARTIN: No, my Lord, but I do want to explain that I don't attach much importance to the nature of a business deal; buy goods, sell goods, sell on commission, commission agreement and so on, etcetera, I lump them all together.

SPELTHORNE, KC: I'll ask you a little about your buying and selling goods in a moment, but first of all, I do want to know if you can give any explanation of how you came to make the mistake.

MARTIN: None at all, except that it isn't the first I've made or the last. The same applies to everyone, I suppose.

SPELTHORNE, KC: The witness you say you're going to call, for instance. Funny he should have made the same mistake.

MARTIN: He didn't, as a matter of fact. He always thought it was March, but I persuaded him out of it. I was sure it was May, and I eventually got him to agree.

SPELTHORNE, KC: Perhaps he didn't think there was an interview at all, and you eventually got him to agree that there was.

MARTIN: Did I catch a note of interrogation in that sentence?

THE JUDGE: Mr Painswick, kindly behave yourself. If you genuinely don't understand a question say so, but don't try to be funny. It will not do you any good.

MARTIN: My Lord, it seems rather hard that I should have to guess whether I am being asked a question. Counsel loves to put in a comment during cross-examination if he gets the chance. Why should I have to sort out the question from the comment? I mean no disrespect, but counsel is quite capable of looking after himself and I'm having to conduct the case myself.

THE JUDGE: I am here to see that you are treated fairly and also that you behave. I hope I shall discharge both duties. Now, don't let's have any more nonsense. Repeat your question, Mr Spelthorne.

SPELTHORNE, KC: Was your witness reluctant to agree that there was an interview until you persuaded him?

MARTIN: Not at all. It was he who reminded me that he was there at all. I'd forgotten.

SPELTHORNE, KC: I thought that the details stood out so well in your memory.

MARTIN: So they have – in the last nine months. Mr Fuller told me a year ago.

SPELTHORNE, KC: Mr Fuller is your witness then?

MARTIN: That's right.

SPELTHORNE, KC: He also happens to be your partner in a firm called Treetop Traders?

MARTIN: Yes.

SPELTHORNE, KC: Not doing very well at the moment, are they?

MARTIN: Unfortunately not. We owe a lot of money.

SPELTHORNE, KC: Any chance of paying it?

MARTIN: I hope so.

SPELTHORNE, KC: If you win this case, I suppose?

MARTIN: Certainly, if I win this case.

SPELTHORNE, KC: That would be a help to your partner, then?

MARTIN: Yes, I suppose, looking at it in that way, it would.

SPELTHORNE, KC: So he can hardly be termed independent.

MARTIN: Isn't that for his Lordship to say? I can only tell you his relationship to me.

SPELTHORNE, KC: Coming back to this interview, can you say on what day of the week it was?

MARTIN: I'm not sure. Could have been a Monday or a Tuesday.

SPELTHORNE, KC: It could have been any day, but I suppose you won't pledge yourself to any day or even any two days?

MARTIN: No, I won't. I'm here to tell the truth.

SPELTHORNE, KC: Yes, that's what you're here for, but are you?

MARTIN: To the best of my ability.

SPELTHORNE, KC: I suggest that the reason you won't pledge yourself to anything but some day in late February or March is that you were so shocked by the passport that you're frightened that, if you commit yourself to the slightest extent, your story will again be upset.

MARTIN: Naturally you put that construction on it, but that is not the case. I don't mind admitting that I was very much shaken by production of the passport. I was sure the interview was in May.

SPELTHORNE, KC: Why are you now sure it was in February or March?

MARTIN: Only because you've proved it wasn't in May, and I know it wasn't later than May or earlier than late February. To be quite frank, I still think it was May, although I know it wasn't, if you follow me.

SPELTHORNE, KC: Now another matter. Yours is a genuine claim according to you, I gather?

MARTIN: Of course. You don't imagine I'd go to this expense and trouble if it wasn't.

SPELTHORNE, KC: It is quite a plain straightforward case?

MARTIN: Absolutely. But, of course, I had nothing in writing.

SPELTHORNE, KC: Is that why you thought it necessary to threaten the defendant?

MARTIN: Threaten? When and in what way? I've demanded my legal rights, that's all.

SPELTHORNE, KC: Just look at the first letter your solicitors wrote when they made the claim on your behalf. What does the last sentence mean?

MARTIN: That I've been corresponding with the USA?

SPELTHORNE, KC: You seem to know what I'm going to ask you. Yes, that's right. What was that about?

MARTIN: I'd rather not say.

SPELTHORNE, KC: But, subject to his Lordship's direction, you must say.

MARTIN: I will if I must, but I don't want to.

THE JUDGE: You will answer the question.

MARTIN: Oh – very well. I was satisfied that Mr Gloster had cheated me out of my commission. It wasn't the first time he'd cheated anybody. I wanted to remind him of what happened to cheats. I'd hoped he'd learned by experience. Do you want any more?

SPELTHORNE, KC: Well?

MARTIN: Do you want any more? I'm not in the least anxious to raise these matters in public. I told you I didn't want to answer your questions about it, but if you want the whole story, I'll give it you. Otherwise I won't say another word about it unless your client swears there was no agreement.

THE JUDGE: Well, Mr Spelthorne, do you wish the witness to go on? He is entitled to, you know, but says he would rather not do so. Do you want him to finish?

SPELTHORNE, KC: I'll put the question another way. Were you not by that sentence threatening the defendant with some kind of exposure if he didn't meet your claim?

MARTIN: It wasn't a threat any more than if I'd said, 'You've done previous people out of their commission and I'm not going to let you do me. Let me remind you in particular of the expense you were put to in trying to evade paying on a previous occasion.' That's all I did, and, if that's wrong, I did wrong. All I can say is that, unless his Lordship tells me not to do so, I shall do it again in similar circumstances. A person who bilks his creditors must expect to be shot at. The remedy is to pay them, as he can well afford to do.

THE JUDGE: Don't make speeches, Mr Painswick.

MARTIN: I'm sorry, my Lord, but being called a blackmailer is very unpleasant.

THE JUDGE: Mr Spelthorne didn't actually use that expression, though I must agree it was implied.

MARTIN: They talk of 'menacing flavour' in their letters, my Lord.

THE JUDGE: Show me. Oh, yes, I see. Yes, Mr Spelthorne, do you wish to ask any more questions about this matter?

SPELTHORNE, KC: I think not, my Lord.

Mr Spratt, who would have been delighted at the way the plaintiff was coming through the witness box if he had still been acting for him, was now as anxious about the case as Mr Toothcombe. Martin, realising what would happen if he threw the slightest blame on his solicitor, had been careful to accept full responsibility himself. In consequence, Mr Spratt could not be of the least use to the defendants. No one would have thought a month or so previously that Mr Spratt and Mr Toothcombe would have lunched together on the first day of the trial and tried to think of some method of breaking Martin down. Mr Spratt would willingly have given in evidence his last conversation with Martin, but such evidence would not have been admissible. It was nothing like so pleasant a lunch as the one they had on the previous occasion.

'He's very clever,' said Mr Spratt.

'Look at his father,' said Mr Toothcombe. 'You'd expect him to be.'

'You see how well he's paved the way for Fuller. I wish I'd had a proof from him. You would have been able to use that somehow. He's only got to go into the witness box and say, "Oh, yes, it was in March, I've always thought it was March, but Mr Painswick was so sure, I thought I must be wrong." How can Spelthorne break that down? I'm afraid you're going to lose this case. It's a fishy story, no date at first, then a wrong month and no documents, but unless one or other of them is broken down, it's a bit difficult for the judge to say there was no interview at all. Then your client can be cross-examined as to credit. I don't like it at all. Do you?'

'I can't say I do, old boy. I wonder if we ought to settle. I'll see what Spelthorne says. But Gloster won't want to and I don't blame him. You and I know he's right. I don't know what I'd do in his place. How much d'you think Painswick would take?'

'Not less than £10,000. I know that's the least that's any use to him.'

'It's the devil of a lot to pay if you don't owe anything.'

Before the resumed hearing the defendant and Mr Toothcombe had a consultation with Mr Spelthorne and Mr Larkins. Mr Spelthorne forecast a victory for the plaintiff. 'It isn't a certainty,' he said, 'and, of course, if I could break Fuller down all would be well. But his part is too easy, and I doubt if I shall. It's up to you, Mr Gloster. I wouldn't pay voluntarily myself if I weren't liable and I believe you when you say you're not, but you're the man who's got to foot the bill and it'll cost you less to settle than to go on and lose.'

Mr Gloster decided to fight. The plaintiff's evidence was accordingly completed and then Fuller gave evidence. He was not such a good witness as Martin, but he had learned his part well and it had certainly been made easy for him. He left the box unshaken. Then Mr Gloster gave evidence. All he could do was to deny the interview, but he had to admit that it was physically possible for him to have been there in February or March.

175

When Martin rose to cross-examine he said: 'I think there's only one question I want to ask you. I'm not the first person you've cheated, am I?'

THE WITNESS: I haven't cheated you. You're trying to cheat me.

MARTIN: Oh – well, I'll have to ask more than one question then. Now, just assume for the purposes of argument that you have cheated me. I wouldn't have been the first, would I?

THE WITNESS: I will not assume any such thing.

MARTIN: I shall have to ask more than two questions. Substitute 'this dispute' for 'cheating me.' Now it will run – you have cheated people before this dispute, haven't you?

THE WITNESS: It depends on what you mean by cheating.

MARTIN: Oh, dear, you are difficult. For the moment I will assume that we both mean the same thing by cheating. Well?

THE WITNESS: Well what?

THE JUDGE: Have you ever cheated anyone before this litigation started?

THE WITNESS: I have been accused of it.

MARTIN: Did you dispute it?

THE WITNESS: I was told that if I pleaded guilty to what was little more than a technical offence, I should only be fined.

MARTIN: So you admitted the technical offence?

THE WITNESS: Yes.

MARTIN: And how much were you fined?

THE WITNESS: I wasn't fined.

MARTIN: Let off altogether?

THE WITNESS: I got twelve months.

MARTIN: Twelve months' imprisonment for the technical offence?

THE WITNESS: Yes.

MARTIN: The technical offence had something to do with cheating, had it not?

THE WITNESS: I don't remember what they called it.

MARTIN: It was worth twelve months, anyway – or perhaps I couldn't expect you to agree to that. That is all I wish to ask, my Lord.

Mr Spelthorne's prophecy came true and, after he had addressed the judge as long as he properly could, judgment was given in favour of the plaintiff. Altogether including the damages for libel, Martin eventually received just over £15,000. In the course of making his £15,000 he had committed at least four crimes – perjury, subornation of perjury, conspiracy and blackmail, a list which must have made his ancestor Uriah look upon him with approbation and consider overlooking the disgrace of having a High Court judge in the family.

CHAPTER SIXTEEN

The System

With this windfall Martin and Mr Fuller managed to arrange their affairs satisfactorily. Mr Spratt had considered going to the police and telling them about Martin's attempts to get him to commit perjury, but there was no witness to the conversation besides the two of them and no other corroboration. He accordingly abandoned the idea with reluctance. In consequence, there was nothing to prevent Martin from enjoying the fruits of his action to the full. Lucy was delighted at the result of the trial, although she had no clear idea of the truth of the matter. Prospects were now much brighter for them – she had known that there were difficulties up to the time of judgment – but now she would be able to bear the first of the next generation of Painswicks in comfort and peace. 'I hope,' said Martin, when she told him she was going to have a baby, 'that it'll be as good a witness as I was.'

Some time later, however, in an action brought against him by a Mr Bright, Martin gave evidence in a much less confident manner than he had exhibited in his action against Mr Gloster. Indeed, so badly did he give evidence that the judge, who tried the case, said to Martin's counsel that he did not believe a word that Martin said where it conflicted with the evidence of the plaintiff. The action was one in which Colin Bright, the plaintiff, had made an excellent impression in the witness box. A pleasant-faced, modest young man, he had spoken with quiet assurance, and cross-examination had only served to increase the value of his evidence. Martin, on the other hand, had been guilty of all the tricks of the shifty, unreliable witness. He might almost have made a study of a really bad liar and imitated him. Now hedging, now trying to be clever, now forced to make a damaging admission, now seeking unsuccessfully to withdraw it, he had been an easy victim for Mr Daniel Feathers, the promising young junior to whom Mr Bright had entrusted his case. It was a case which had attracted a good deal of attention and was of particular interest to the sporting public. Mr Bright claimed that, while in the Army, he had during his spare time, developed a system for backing horses which he had thought at least worth a trial. He said that, on being demobilised, he had taken up employment at a salary which was insufficient for the purpose of trying out the system. This did not require much capital – about a hundred pounds – but it was more than he could manage. One day he happened to meet Martin and casually mentioned the matter to him. The latter showed a great interest and eventually, according to the evidence of the plaintiff, an agreement was made between them by which the plaintiff was to explain the system to the defendant, the defendant was to put it into operation, to pay all losses and to give one-third of the profits (if any) to the plaintiff. Mr Bright alleged that Martin had used the system with great good fortune, but that, apart from about £200 which he paid him in the first flush of success, he had refused to pay him his share. Many members of the public had thought that such an agreement as was alleged to have been made between the parties in this case was binding in honour only, like a bet. They learned, however, that they were wrong. As Mr Justice Pennant stated in his judgment, the law is that, while a bet is unenforceable, nevertheless, if a man makes a successful bet on behalf of someone else and receives the winnings, he is legally liable to hand over the amount he has received to the person on whose behalf he made the bet. He cannot, of course, be sued if he does not make the bet or if the bookmaker does not pay, but only if he receives the winnings. So in *Bright v Painswick*, if the plaintiff's story was right and if Martin had received large sums as a result of the use of the system, the plaintiff was entitled to one-third of the profits. There was no dispute that this was the law, but Martin raised various defences. First of all, he denied that any agreement was made. He said it was only a vague arrangement. Then he said that, if (which was denied) any agreement was made, £200 was the total amount due to the plaintiff. In case that defence should fail, he said that any profits for which he had not accounted had not been made as a result of using the system. Finally, he said that, if all these defences failed, he had, in fact, paid to the plaintiff £15,000 in £1 notes, which was exactly one-third of the profits he had made, if he had made any (which he denied). Lawyers are used to alternative and inconsistent defences and frequently the use of them does not in any way prejudice a defendant. In the present case, however, Martin's inconsistent stories told heavily against him. Although the evidence had to be extracted from him bit by bit and at the cost of considerable persistence by Mr Feathers and of equal apparent discomfiture to the witness, in the end he was forced to admit that he had received vast sums from bookmakers. It eventually seemed clear to any impartial observer that Martin was attempting to bilk Mr Bright, that his various inconsistent stories were all untrue and that he did in fact owe Mr Bright a very large sum of money indeed. It was when Martin's counsel was endeavouring to find something to say on his client's behalf that the judge said that he rejected the whole of Martin's evidence where it conflicted with the plaintiff's. Counsel did not keep it up much longer after that, and a few minutes later judgment was being delivered. In the course of a short judgment the judge said, among other things: 'It is not for this Court to enquire into the usefulness or otherwise of the plaintiff's system to the world at large in its present difficulties. I am not concerned with morals nor with the way in which people make their money, provided it is lawfully made. Moreover, one must accept as a fact that a very large portion of the community does amuse itself in the usually unprofitable pastime of backing horses. The plaintiff while rendering great service to his country during the war, invented the system which is the subject-matter of this action. It has not been necessary for the purpose of deciding this case to make public the details of that system, and I have no doubt but that bookmakers as a class must be very grateful that I did not find it necessary to do so. Perhaps I should add, to prevent any false impressions, that, although the plaintiff has put the system into writing and I glanced through a copy, it was not necessary for me to understand it, still less to memorise it, and I did not do either. I am quite satisfied,' he went on, 'that a binding agreement was made between the parties, that the use of the system resulted in a profit of at least £45,000, and that, apart from £200, no part of this has been paid to the plaintiff. I accordingly give judgment for the plaintiff for £14,800 with costs.'

Outside the Court, after there had been exchanged the usual congratulations between the plaintiff and his legal advisers and the usual condolences between Martin and his legal advisers, Mr Bright was approached by a member of the press who asked him to interview his Editor. He assented, and a day or two later was sitting with the Editor of the *Sporting Sun*.

'I'm afraid not,' he was saying. 'I agree that £50 a week is good pay, but now that the case has shown that the system has some value, I think I should like to sell it for a capital sum. Besides,' he added, 'the system isn't foolproof by any means, and, if your readers misused it, you might want to terminate my contract.'

In spite of an increased offer, he maintained this attitude and even several drinks at a Fleet Street tavern failed to make him change his mind. The Editor went back to his office defeated, and he was in no way comforted by hearing on his return that an absolutely certain thing for the four o'clock had come in second by a short head.

Within the next week Mr Bright received thousands of letters, the majority from regular backers, but quite a fair number, from men and women (and schoolboys) who had never even backed a horse before. The letters made offers of various kinds and some enclosed cheques and cash in advance. This was only to be expected, but Mr Bright was a little surprised at the number of applicants for initiation into the system and the classes of the population from which they came. Some were almost illiterate, there was a ducal coronet on one and several came from schoolmasters or university professors. A few politicians were included, but no member of the Liberal party wrote in his own name. He was a little astonished at the number which came from women. There were also, of course, a number of letters of abuse and a few requests for temporary financial assistance. Mr Bright engaged a secretary to sort the letters and eventually hired a hall and called a meeting of a selected audience of about a thousand. He addressed them in the pleasant modest manner he had displayed in the witness box.

'Ladies and gentlemen,' he said. 'I thought it easier to answer your letters in this way and I much appreciate your kindness in coming – some of you from quite a long way.' (By the time the meeting took place, he had had wires from Australia and the United States.) 'What I have to tell you today is quite simple. I claim no infallibility for my system. In my humble opinion, there is no such thing as an infallible system. I did, however, spend quite a lot of time in writing it, and I am bound to say that I was very pleased at the result of my recent action before Mr Justice Pennant. You all apparently want to buy this system from me. I am quite prepared to sell it to a number of you, but I think it only right that the number should be limited. Accordingly, my offer to you is this; I will give a copy of the system to the first five hundred of you to send me £50 each. I will undertake not to disclose the system to anyone else, and if more than five hundred cheques are received, the first five hundred letters to be opened will be selected and the remaining cheques returned.'

The price did not seem unreasonable, and the feeling of the meeting was obviously favourable. With disarming and characteristic modesty, Mr Bright went on: 'I do not ask you to buy it, I give no warranty with it, and I make no representation about it. I don't suggest that it is any better than any of those systems which are advertised regularly in the sporting press, but if you want it, you shall have it.'

They did want it, and they had it. Mr Bright cashed five hundred cheques for £50 each and sent to each of the drawers a copy of the system. It was a somewhat lengthy document, and it was obviously written by Mr Bright, as one could see the same pleasant modest style of writing as he had used in speaking. It went into the matter of backing horses in considerable detail, but, to summarise it, it advised the reader to study carefully the breeding and form of the horses, to make sure which horses were running in a race and what the betting was before making a bet, and to give due effect to the weight each horse was carrying. For instance, with regard to breeding, it pointed out that in a sprint race it was a good thing to back a horse sired by Gold Bridge unless, of course, there was also running in the same race a horse sired by Fair Trial or Denturius or Panorama, or one of a number of other sires. It advised the purchase of numerous books (including the *Bloodstock Breeders' Review* and other expensive volumes). It pointed out that a horse could not run successfully in a long race unless it had stayers' blood in it, and it gave an excellent list of staying sires. It quoted numerous examples to prove its point. It was not uninteresting, and was even entertaining on occasions, but none of it was in the least new or original. If you read the whole of it, you could not avoid the conclusion that the stay-at-home backer can never hope to win in the long run unless he subscribes to an information service giving him full particulars of each race before it is run. It also seemed reasonably plain that, even then, he can never hope to win unless he spends most of the hours of each day studying form and breeding and has no other occupation to distract him. The same, of course, applied to the regular race-goer. Professional backers who read it threw it aside in disgust and wrote off the £50 as a lost bet. The opinions of amateurs varied. Some were intrigued, bought some of the books, studied breeding and form, subscribed to an information service, spent a lot of time and lost a lot of money. Others were appalled at the labour involved and dropped the whole idea. Others, still, gave it a trial and, after much labour, won the little money they would have won more easily by following 'Tipster' of the *Sporting Sun*. With the exception of the few (very few) in the last class, they all eventually came to the conclusion that they had been 'had,' though they were bound to admit that no false representation had been made by Mr Bright about his system. If, however, they had seen Mr Bright and Martin drinking champagne together just after they had cashed the five hundred cheques for £50 each, they would have thought very differently, but it need hardly be added that meetings between Martin and Mr Bright were very discreetly arranged.

Although, however, this fraud was never discovered, the proceeds of it did not last for ever, and the time came when Martin had again to call in aid his inventive powers. He was incapable of using them honestly, and it is very difficult to live almost entirely from dishonesty. If he could only have been satisfied with the results of one or two successful crimes, he might never have been convicted, but he just did not know when to stop. In consequence, the day eventually came when he found himself in the dock at the Old Bailey with a defence which he correctly anticipated that the jury would not accept.

'It is a great sorrow to me,' said Mr Justice Drone, 'to have to pass sentence upon the son of so distinguished a father.'

'Do leave my father out of it,' said Martin.

'It must be a bitter blow to him,' went on the judge.

'Then don't rub the wound,' said Martin.

'If you do not keep quiet while I pass sentence,' said the judge, 'I will adjourn the case to next session and do so then. That would mean an extra month for you in prison.'

He went on for some time and ended with 'three years' imprisonment.'

So Martin went off to Wormwood Scrubs prison. He quickly picked up the routine there, and after a few days he lodged a notice of appeal and asked his father to come and see him.

Mr Justice Painswick had taken the blow as well as could be expected. It was not a surprise, but none the easier to bear because of that. Still, there was nothing he could do about it and he was glad, at any rate, that Lucy took it so well. He saw her and his grandchild from time to time and they arranged to spend the weekend after Martin's conviction at the vicarage. The vicar was now very much better, but he had been forced to retire and was living very happily with Caroline in a transformed vicarage.

Before the weekend the judge went to see Martin. They were allowed to see each other alone in a consultation room.

'Sorry about this, father,' said Martin. 'It was careless of me. I wish I hadn't let you down. I'm not worried about Lucy and the boy. They'll be all right, and it'll be quite good for them to have me out of the way for a bit. What do your brother judges say to you? Nothing like that old fool Drone, I hope. I could have thrown something at him.'

'As a matter of fact he wrote me a very charming letter. They're all very kind and it doesn't really affect me personally – but I can't feel exactly pleased about it. However, I suppose I have to be resigned to having a scapegrace for a son. Is there anything I can do for him?'

'Nothing, father, thanks, except cheer up. Oh, no, there is one thing. I owe a few pounds to a chap. I'll give you his name and address. D'you mind paying him? It's only three pounds ten. It's quite near you, actually, but you can just post it. I'll pay you back when I come out, but he can't afford to be without the money. Just put a note, "From Martin Painswick" in it. That's all.'

'All right,' said the judge. 'Who and where is it?'

Martin gave him the name and address and they went on to discuss other matters. Eventually the interview closed and the judge left the prison. Martin immediately withdrew his notice of appeal.

The address given by Martin was so near to the judge's home that he decided to deliver the money in person. He called at the house and asked for Mr Brown.

'That's me,' said the man who opened the door.

'I have three pounds ten from Martin Painswick for you.'

'OK. Hop it.'

The man took the money from the judge and immediately slammed the door in his face. The judge did not have to wait long to learn the cause of this extraordinary behaviour. He had just started to walk away from the house when two men approached him.

'Like a word with you,' one of them said.

'Indeed,' said the judge. 'Who are you?'

'Detective-Sergeant Collie of the CID. I'd like you to come to the station and give me some information, please.'

The judge was now feeling a little uncomfortable. The behaviour of Mr Brown and the immediate arrival of two detectives made it almost certain that there was something wrong with the three pounds ten transaction. He was a completely innocent party in the matter, but having regard to his son's recent conviction, it was an unpleasant position to be in.

'I will give you any information you want at my flat,' he said, 'as soon as you've established your identity. I am a

High Court judge, Sir Charles Painswick, and I will show you my identity card now if you wish.'

Both men started and looked at each other. Then Sergeant Collie said: 'I'm extremely sorry to trouble you, Sir Charles. I had no idea. It's very good of your Lordship to help us, and I'd be grateful if you'd see us in your flat. Here is my warrant card. This is Detective-Sergeant Owen.'

They walked to the judge's flat.

'Now, what can I do for you?' he said as soon as they were in the sitting-room.

'It's a little embarrassing, sir,' said Sergeant Collie. 'I'm sure you'll realise we're only doing our duty and mean no disrespect.'

'Of course,' said the judge. 'Go on.'

'We were keeping observation on the house where you called.'

'Yes.'

'We saw you give something to the man who opened the door. Would you mind telling us what it was?'

'Certainly not. It was three pounds ten which my son had asked me to give to Mr Brown. It was repayment of a loan.'

'I'm sorry to have to ask this, sir, but do you mean your son who was recently convicted?'

'I do.'

'And is now in Woodworm Scrubs prison?'

'Yes.'

'May I ask when you saw him?'

'Today. Now do you mind telling me what this is all about?'

'Yes, sir. I think we'd better. And if I may say so with the greatest respect, I shouldn't carry out any more commissions of that sort for your son.'

'What d'you mean? Wasn't it repayment of a loan?'

'It certainly wasn't. You may not know, sir, that there is a tobacco racket at most prisons. Money is paid to someone outside the prison and tobacco finds its way inside. Those in the know get a regular ration that way. But no pay, no tobacco. It works like clockwork and it's very difficult to detect for reasons which you'll understand. I'm surprised at your son asking you to do it for him, if I may say so.'

'He did suggest I should post it.'

'That was considerate of him, anyway. Well now, sir, are you prepared to sign a statement? I do realise how awkward it is for you, sir, but I must, at any rate, ask you. I can't force you to give one, sir, if you take my meaning. And, of course, it goes without saying that your word will be accepted as to what happened.'

'Thank you,' said the judge. 'It's nice to know that.'

'It's lucky, really, it was you and not his wife, sir. It wouldn't have been so easy for her.'

'I think,' said the judge, 'I ought to give you a signed statement, and I will do so. Should it involve my having to give evidence that will be my misfortune, but not your fault.'

Sergeant Collie accordingly took down the judge's statement and the judge signed it. Soon after they left.

'I don't suppose we'll get a chance of knocking off a High Court judge again,' he said to his companion. 'I'm keeping a note of this for my reminiscences.'

CHAPTER SEVENTEEN

Certainty

On the following Friday the judge caught a train for
Poppleton. Just before the train started a middle-aged
man got in and sat opposite to him. They looked at each
other and it was obvious that they felt they had met
before. Each of them looked out of the window and
thought. Suddenly the judge's companion said: 'I know
– Painswick. You're a judge now. Remember me? I'm
Melton.'

'Good gracious, yes, of course. I couldn't think who you
were. It's a long time ago, but you haven't changed,
really.'

Mr Justice Painswick and Professor Melton had read law
together at Cambridge, but they had hardly ever seen each
other since. The judge had succeeded at the practical side
of the law and the professor at the academic. He now had
the Chair of Jurisprudence at Cambridge, and his books
on the subject were held in great esteem by lawyers all over
the English-speaking world.

'How have things been going with you?' asked the
judge.

'Oh, very well, thank you. I was at Harvard for a time,
you know, and then I came back to Cambridge, a year or
two back.'

'Married?'

'No. A confirmed bachelor. And you?'

'A widower.'

'Any children?'

'Yes, a son.'

'Has he followed in your footsteps?'

The judge hesitated. 'I'm afraid not. He's been rather a disappointment to me.'

'Oh, I'm sorry. I imagine you expected too much of him. What's he doing now?'

'I gather you don't read the papers very much.'

'I see *The Times*, you know.'

'Well, if you'd read that carefully, you'd have known what he was doing, I'm afraid. There's no point in beating about the bush. He's doing three years at the moment. Just starting.'

'Bless my soul. I'm terribly sorry. But now I do remember. I did read about it. It was rather a clever fraud on estate agents, wasn't it?'

'Something of the kind.'

'Most ingenious. Serve them right, anyway. Stupid lot of people. If you want to sell a house – "Prices aren't what they were. I think I should ask less than that, sir." If you want to buy one – " Oh, you'll never get it for that, sir, prices are soaring at the moment." All on the same day, too. And then the agreements they draw – and charge for too. A law student who failed in Real Property could do better. In my view, it's a fraud on the public to let estate agents draw agreements, let alone charge for them. Sorry about the three years, though. It must be a blow.'

'It is. I'm fond of the boy, and it's a shame he's turned out as he has. He's quite bright, you know. Would have done well at the Bar. Married quite a nice girl. They're very happy and I'm a grandfather; I won't say a proud grandfather in the circumstances, but still a grandfather.'

'Well, you look very well on it.'

They lapsed into silence for a short time; then the professor asked the judge where he was going.

'As a matter of fact I'm just going to see my daughter-in-law. She's staying with her parents in a little village near Poppleton called Tapworth Magna.'

'Tapworth, Tapworth?' said the professor. 'I seem to have heard the name.'

'I expect you saw it in the papers some years ago. My boy's father-in-law used to be the vicar there. You probably read about him. There was a great stir about his insight into horse racing.'

'You must mean old Meeson-Smith?'

'Yes, d'you know him?'

'Oh, no, but I knew of him at the time. I don't think, though, that that's the Tapworth I'm thinking of. Funny, I just can't place it. I expect it will come back to me. Oh, yes, I read all about old Meeson-Smith. I'm very keen on racing, you know. I lose quite a lot each year, all of £100.'

'That seems rather foolish.'

'Why indeed? It amuses me. You probably spend as much on something else – cigarettes, for instance. Now I don't smoke. Why shouldn't I back horses instead? I never lose more than I can afford, and occasionally I win. You'd be amazed if you knew the number of people who did the same. It wouldn't in the least surprise me if you told me you did. But I suppose you'll say you've never been on a racecourse.'

'Only twice.'

'Didn't you enjoy it?'

'It was a new experience, but I can't say that I particularly enjoyed it.'

'Lose much?'

'No.'

'Make anything?'

'Well yes.'

'Wise man, stick to your winnings. I could never do it. Shouldn't want to either. Nobody who thinks ever expects to make any money by betting. But there aren't many people who do think. Fortunately for the bookmakers. They try all sorts of infallible systems which always break down. You haven't the slightest hope of success unless, of course, you're a multi-millionaire and don't need the money. Such a man, I suppose, by investing half a crown in the first instance and contenting himself with a total win of about twelve and sixpence a week could be certain of making money. The only way of making real money is by finding the winner, and no one can do that often enough. Wait a moment, though. Two or three years ago the *Daily Echo* did find a man who could pick winners with unfailing regularity. Much good it did them. They had to get rid of him after a year.'

'How was that?'

'I'll tell you. It was a man who called himself "Certainty." A good name, and he lived up to it. I remember now. It wasn't long after old Meeson-Smith came into prominence. The *Daily Echo* suddenly came out with this tipster "Certainty." They said they'd taken him on because he had proved to them over the previous two months that he could give one certain winner a week. "IN EIGHT WEEKS EIGHT WINNERS," ran the headline introducing "Certainty" to the readers of the *Daily Echo*. They didn't take much notice of him the first week, but he gave a winner at long odds. The second week he gave another winner at 10 to 1. The third week he had a bigger following. In the face of a strong odds-on favourite he gave another horse. It won at 5 to 1. By this time "Certainty" was becoming known, while the editorial staff on the *Daily Echo*, who had now seen him give eleven winners in succession, proceeded to back him heavily themselves. The fourth week he gave a winner which wasn't mentioned by another tipster. In the betting forecast it was put among the 20 to 1 others. It ran and won at 2 to 1. You can see what's going to happen. The week after, his horse won at even money. The week after that at odds on. After that, "Certainty's" winners of the week were backed by nearly every betting reader of the *Daily Echo*, and by many of their friends. The circulation of the paper soared to the skies. Within a month or two "Certainty's" horse ran at 10 to 1 on. Even that didn't stop them. If it really was a certainty there was no risk. After six months, "Certainty's" horse never ran at less than 33 to 1 on. Then one day at 50 to 1 on – mark you, he had had over twenty-five successive winners – so you can't blame the bookmakers – it slipped and fell when it would otherwise have won. Even that didn't stop them. They doubled and trebled their stakes next time and made a little money at 25 to 1 on. It's incredible to think of it. Even if it had never fallen and always won, the odds were so prohibitive that it's amazing that people thought it worthwhile. They made so little, though, that "Certainty's" horses became a joke. The small backer could only win a few pence. The heavy backer could only win a few pounds. Still they went on backing them. It was the owners and trainers who eventually put a stop to it.'

'How was that?'

'I'll tell you. You might see a list of fifteen probables. As soon as "Certainty" gave one of them as the winner, half of them would withdraw. Then three-quarters. No use running a horse in a race if it's no chance. Eventually all of them withdrew, so that "Certainty's" horse always had a walk-over, except in the Classic races, and there are only five of them. So that was the end of "Certainty." What I never understood was why he wrote for the press instead of betting himself. He must have had a big fan mail. And think of the offers that must have been made to him.'

'Very interesting,' said the judge. 'It sounds as though the vicar had a rival. They would have done well together.'

Not long afterwards they arrived at Poppleton and the judge left the professor still trying to remember his association with Tapworth.

Lucy met the judge at the station and chatted cheerfully to him during the drive to the vicarage.

'It's like someone being away at the war – only much safer,' she said. 'Won't it be lovely when he comes out? I count the days like I did at boarding school.'

'Martin's a very lucky man to have you,' said the judge.

'Well, I think I'm lucky to have Martin. Not everyone has a judge for a father-in-law.'

At the vicarage he was made very welcome. Later on in the course of conversation he mentioned his meeting with the professor. 'Do you know if there's another Tapworth anywhere? He seemed so puzzled about it.'

'I've never heard of one,' said the vicar. 'Perhaps it was just one of those tricks of the mind which make you think you've heard something before when, in fact, you haven't.'

'Perhaps so, vicar. Oh, there's another thing that will interest you. He told me about a racing tipster some year or two ago, who seemed to be as good as you. What was his name – not "Surety" – '

' "Certainty"?' said the vicar.

'That was it. You've heard of him, I gather.'

'Yes,' said the vicar, 'he was as good as me, exactly and precisely as good as me. You might as well say it was me, and it was.'

'But I thought – '

'You're shocked, horrified. I'm very pleased you are. I should have been upset if you hadn't been. But it's all right. You needn't be. It suddenly occurred to me what fun I could have. I knew exactly what must happen, and, of course, it did, though it took a little longer than I expected. I had retired, you know, at the time, and it's only fair to tell you that I took nothing for it. I thought it a very pleasant practical joke. Rather a paradox, don't you think? If a paper gives too many losers, its readers complain. If it gives too many winners, they stop reading it altogether. No, racing will only continue while people lose money. I could, if I chose, stop racing altogether. I have proved that by my career as "Certainty." However, I don't feel called upon to do that, but it amused me to show that it could be done.'

'But didn't it start the same business all over again? Wasn't Tapworth Magna invaded for a second time?'

'Oh, no, I was too careful. I got Caroline to arrange it through a friend in town. No one knew I was behind it. We had many a good laugh over it. As a matter of fact, I was rather naughty at the end of my career. I could see the end almost in sight. Well, there was a £200 selling plate and there was a sweet old mare in it called My Darling Caroline. Very like the original. It was seven years old. It had been quite a good sprinter in its day, but had gradually gone down and down (unlike the original) until the best it could do was to go in for small selling plates. Well, I was sorry for this old mare, and wanted to see it win one race for its owner. It had, in fact, no chance of winning if there was any other horse in the race, but I gave it as the horse for the week and all the others duly scratched. I am not sure about the morality of it, but I satisfied my conscience in two ways. First, I wasn't paid for it; and secondly, after all, I did give the winner, didn't I?'

'You certainly did. And no one will ever be able to prove it wouldn't have won.'

Later the vicar referred to Martin. 'I am deeply distressed for you,' he said, 'and I am glad that to some extent I can share your sorrow. Lucy is very dear to us, and her unhappiness is ours too.'

'She is remarkably cheerful,' said the judge. 'If I did not know how attached they were to each other I should have imagined that she was pleased.'

'She has always made the best of things. We've tried to bring her up that way. At one time we had quite a struggle here – for existence, I mean, but Lucy was always cheerful. So were we all. My darling Caroline not the least. And then we had that stroke of good fortune just when I was taken ill. I often wish that I could find the anonymous donor. I could tell him of our immeasurable thankfulness and of the help it has been to us. Before my illness things were difficult but we could manage, but afterwards life would have been grim indeed but for this benefaction. I wish he could see how happy he has made us. He must be a good man, and I am sure it would make his heart rejoice.'

The vicar had quite a strong feeling that the judge was the person in question. Caroline intervened to save him embarrassment.

'You say a man, dear, but it might have been a woman. The solicitors may have said "he" to prevent our finding out.'

'True, my dear, but I don't know why, I think it was a man.'

197

In this he differed from the Bishop's wife.

The weekend passed very pleasantly in spite of the occasion of the visit. Lady Brain (formerly Mrs Poulter) brought her fourth husband to tea on the Sunday.

'I've brought round Hugo for you to look at, vicar,' she said. 'What d'you think of him?'

Sir Hugo twirled his moustaches.

'My wife,' he said, 'usually refers to me as if I were a picture. Would you like to take me over to the light?'

'I'm delighted to meet you, sir,' said the vicar. 'I hope that you will be very happy.' He did not add 'but doubt it.' He then introduced him to the judge.

'Hugo was a great athlete in his day, vicar. He ran for England,' said his wife.

'Indeed,' said the judge. 'You must be H F Brain, the miler.'

'Guilty, my Lord,' said Sir Hugo, 'but I ask for leniency. It was a long time ago, and I've done nothing of the sort since then.'

'He's done nothing of any sort,' put in his wife. 'He's very rich.'

'I married you. Is that nothing?'

'Oh, I meant before that. Would you believe it, I'm the first woman to lead him to matrimony.'

'Push and shove, more like,' commented Sir Hugo. 'I've never been so bullied in my life. Can't think why I stood for it. I like it well enough though. Still, there's plenty of time yet. Only been married a week.'

'He's seventy-six,' said his wife. 'He doesn't look it, does he?'

'Remarkable,' said the vicar. 'Seventy-six.'

'His heart's not too strong, though.'

'That's a legacy of your running days, I suppose?'

'Sound as a bell, sir. Don't take any notice of my wife. She's an incurable optimist, but I'll show her. Long-lived family the Brains. Father lived to ninety-five, mother to ninety-four. No, no tea, thank you. You haven't a drop of brandy in the house, I suppose?'

'We've sal volatile, I know,' said the vicar. 'Do you feel faint?'

'Good gracious, no. Just don't care for tea, that's all. Let it pass.'

'Of course we have some brandy,' said Caroline, 'I'll get some.'

'Oh, pray, don't trouble. Oh, well, if you insist. Only a thimbleful. Two fingers or so.'

CHAPTER EIGHTEEN

Generation Succeeds Generation

That night Mr Justice Painswick lay awake for a long time thinking about his past. He went right back to his childhood, lived swiftly through his schooldays, went back to Cambridge and was called to the Bar. He was wondering what mistake he had made and when he had made it, and he examined critically the various periods of his life for this purpose. He assumed that Martin's downfall must in some way be due to some lapse on his part. 'I suppose,' he said to himself, 'most of the things that happen to a man must in great measure depend on his object in life. What was mine?' That was a question which he did not find it easy to answer, and many people would have a similar difficulty. The existence of that difficulty is enough by itself to account for failure. Any commanding officer would rightly say that to have any reasonable chance of success a plan must have a clearly defined and simply expressed object. Is it to capture the hill or kill the enemy that holds it? It may be possible to do both, but if it is not, which takes pride of place? It is no good attacking until you know. 'What was my object in life?' thought the judge. 'To be successful? To be happy? To make other people happy? All three when possible, but if they clashed, which was to come first? Success and happiness may go together and often do, but not always. Which did I want the more?' he asked himself. 'To make other people happy may make a man very happy himself, but not always; sometimes the reverse. What was my main object?' he thought. He argued with himself on the subject as honestly as possible, but he could come to no clear conclusion for some time. Finally he decided that his main object had been to be happy. Had he gone the right way about securing happiness for himself? If success took second place when it clashed with happiness, why had he devoted so much time to his work and so little to bringing up Martin? He remembered his first days at the Bar when briefs were few and very small, though they sounded most important when he spoke of them to friends or acquaintances.

'Are you a barrister?' says the sweet young thing. 'Oh, how thrilling. Have you done many murder cases?' *Many* murder cases! The nearest approach to a murder case with which the young Painswick, barrister-at-law, had been called upon to deal was an inquest upon an unfortunate man who had been knocked down accidentally by a lorry. But he made the most of that and of the claim for £7 3s 4d for goods sold and delivered before His Honour Judge Smoothe, who had congratulated him on the way in which he had presented his case. He had most unfortunately lost it, but of course it was one in which nobody could have succeeded for his client. He brushed aside (not only when telling the story but temporarily, at any rate, in his own mind) the fact that he had omitted to quote to the judge an authority which would have compelled a decision in his client's favour. He didn't mention that his client had suggested (curiously enough, in the most friendly manner) that next time he might equip himself with the latest textbook on the subject. Such experiences and many others beside he remembered and related with gusto later on when he had acquired a large and lucrative practice. He could afford to do so then. It is curious how interested the general public is in the law and the lawyers. Doctors, no doubt, when gathered together, talk medicine to each other as much as lawyers talk law. But what interest does the doctor evoke among laymen when he says, 'I once treated a man who had an arthritic cyst in the acromio-clavicular joint'? Who wants to hear about cysts, arthritic or otherwise (unless the listener has one himself), or acromio-clavicular joints? House-breaking, burglary, even petty larceny, on the other hand, are very different matters, though few (if any) of the audience have been guilty of any of these crimes. But in spite of the advantage it gives to the young member of the Bar at parties, the judge had not gone to the criminal Bar. In his very early days he did a few criminal cases, but when at last his real worth began to assert itself, he practised almost entirely in commercial law. What a struggle it had been at first, and what appalling labour later on. Everything was sacrificed to his practice – wife, son, friends, amusements, everything else. There is probably no harder worked person than the moderately or very successful barrister at the commercial or common law Bar. No free evenings or weekends for him. 'I wanted happiness,' thought the judge. 'If I had devoted less time to work and given time to watching Martin's development and assisting it when necessary, I should have found much more. Yet would I? Perhaps it was heredity which was too strong. Well, I shall never know. I've had success, yes – and enjoyed it. But that didn't keep my wife alive nor save Martin from prison. Would I act differently if I started all over again?' So he went on, worrying over something for which neither worry nor anything else was a remedy. At last he fell asleep and a week after he woke up he became a Lord Justice of Appeal.

Rather more than two years after he woke up he met Martin on his release from prison. Lucy went with him. She had no illusions about Martin and did not think for a moment that he would have learned his lesson and gone straight (as not being found out is normally called) in the future. She knew he would not be able to avoid committing crimes or being caught. She simply hoped that he would be at home as long as possible. She told this to the judge on their way to meet him. Martin soon proved her to be right. He was extremely cheerful, but quite unrepentant on his release. He was delighted to see his father and very apologetic about the tobacco incident, but he made it quite clear that his sentence had only determined him to be more careful in the future.

'I'm so very sorry,' he said, 'but it's no good. I shall always be the same. Anyway, it makes for variety in the family. Cheer up, father, let's go and have a drink.'

For a short time after his release Martin did, in fact, lead an honest life. This was not from any change of heart on his part, but simply because he was not quite ready to begin work again. He wanted some rest and amusement and he had both first. Then the time came when, in his words, he had to put his shoulder to the wheel again, but he did not find it quite so easy. Once a conviction has been recorded against you, you will find it far more difficult to live a life of crime successfully. This particularly applied to the type of fraud practised by Martin. For instance, it would have been quite impossible for him to indulge in any further fraudulent litigation unless his name were kept out of it. Then again, the police are far more eager to deal with a complaint of fraud if they know that the person against whom the complaint is made has been convicted before. Martin realised this fairly well before he went to work again, but by the end of his career he knew it very well indeed. However, his motto in life had always been that difficulties were made to be overcome, and in spite of the obstacles in the way of his success, he managed to perpetrate a large number of ingenious and lucrative frauds. They were, however, more often than not discovered in the end, and though by the time of his arrest he had usually managed to put away sufficient of the proceeds to provide quite a satisfactory income, he began to find the years he was spending in prison outnumbering the years he was able to spend with Lucy. His first sentence had been three years. His next was four. Shortly after his release from that sentence his father died. The judge had never lost his affection for Martin who, in his own way, returned it. After he had read the eulogistic obituaries in the Press praising Lord Justice Painswick's judicial sense, his knowledge of the law, his fairness and courtesy and stating baldly at the end that he had had one son, Martin decided to keep out of prison for at least a year.

'People thought a lot of the old man,' he said to Lucy, 'and quite rightly too. It would be a shame to follow up these notices with another of the "Martin Painswick, described as an accountant, was charged at ..." No, we'll have to go carefully for a bit. I shan't be able to manage that new fur coat at present, if you don't mind.' He gave it her eighteen months later, and six months afterwards 'Martin Painswick, described as an accountant,' went to prison for another three years. This was his third conviction, and after several more, he received a sentence of preventive detention.

By the time he was eighty he calculated that he had spent about a third of his life in prison.

'You grow older but no better,' said a judge, who knew him well, when sentencing him on his seventy-fifth birthday.

'Much worse, my Lord,' said Martin. 'I should never have been caught for this twenty years ago. I won't say I'm getting out of practice, but I have a nasty feeling that my hand is losing its cunning.'

'I should think that over during the next five years,' said the judge.

'I think I will, my Lord,' said Martin. 'I'm grateful to your Lordship for giving me the opportunity.'

He did think it over, and he finally came to the conclusion that, if he were ever caught again, he would retire. Lucy tried to persuade him to do so on his release, but he said he wanted 'to have one more go.' 'Just an old man's fancy,' he said.

CHAPTER NINETEEN

And So On

In consequence, towards his eighty-fourth birthday, Martin appeared at his local quarter sessions charged with obtaining money by false pretences. It was a comparatively petty fraud. He pleaded guilty and, on being asked if he had anything to say, he said this: 'Sir, I have never previously asked any Court for leniency, and I think I can fairly say that I have not been shown, or for that matter deserved, any. I do not pretend that I deserve any now, but I have something important to tell you which may affect your mind when you come to pass sentence. I have never yet told a lie in Court, except, of course, in the witness box. As long as I was pleading "Not guilty" I felt justified in bolstering up my plea with such evidence as I thought would be most effective. Once convicted, however, I have never made promises of reformation, and I can truthfully say that up to date I have never reformed. My first sentence was one of three years' imprisonment. I do not pretend that it was too long or, indeed, that it was not overdue. When convicted on that occasion I made no plea for mercy or promise of better behaviour. I did not intend to behave any better when I had served my sentence and I certainly did not do so. I have been in and out of prison ever since then, and I am now an old man of eighty-four.

I have noticed in the last years that my brain is not so active as it was and that my inventive powers, which used to be considerable, are deteriorating. I am heartily ashamed of my present offence. It is the first time I have been ashamed of anything, though I admit that I have from time to time been displeased at being found out. I hope I shall not be considered to be too conceited if I say that the present offence was wholly unworthy of me. Now what is all this leading up to? It is this: I have decided to retire. I think it is time I made way for a younger man. If I go on as I am I shall most probably die in prison, which neither my wife nor I would like. We have been married very nearly fifty years. In fact, we shall celebrate (if you give us the chance) our golden wedding on Thursday. If the offence to which I have pleaded "Guilty" had been a first offence, I think it is not unreasonable to assume I might well have been given another chance. Now in the past – quite rightly – I have never been given another chance. I should not have taken it. This time, I assure you I will. I go further. Even if you send me to prison I shall retire when I come out – if I do come out. Now, in all these circumstances, I do ask you to accept my word and for the first time in my criminal career to bind me over. No one will be any the worse off. It will not encourage criminals elsewhere. On the other hand, my wife and I will be much better off and I venture to think that when you, sir, and your fellow magistrates go back to your families it will give you a little sentimental pleasure to think that the old man and his wife are spending their golden wedding together.'

The power of advocacy, which Martin had inherited from his father, had never been more effectively used. Two hours later he was back with his wife, drinking a toast to his release. Before making his decision Lucy and he had carefully weighed up the matter and they had found that they had sufficient savings to enable them to live in comparative comfort for the rest of their years.

'It will be quite a change,' said Lucy, 'not having to wonder if the next knock on the door is a policeman's.'

There was a knock at the door immediately afterwards. They were not yet out of the habit, and automatically Martin wondered which particular crime was being brought home to him. Indeed, for the first time since he arrived home their faces fell. They had been looking forward to a period of uninterrupted happiness. The caller must have noticed this for, as soon as he had been let in, he said: 'It's all right, I'm only from the *Echo*. Hope you don't mind my calling.'

The old couple were so relieved that they laughed with pleasure.

'Come in, come in,' said Martin. 'Join us in a glass of sherry.'

'Thank you very much.'

The journalist took his glass and drank to his host and hostess.

'That was a very good speech of yours,' he said. 'I'm writing you up in the *Echo*, and I wondered if you'd give me a story or two.'

'Anything to help,' said Martin. 'May I say that we are so grateful to you for not being a policeman that I feel I owe it to you? Not that there's anything on my mind (I don't say "conscience") at the moment, but we're so used to these knocks, you know, it'll take a bit of time before they don't make us start.'

'Quite so, very sorry to have worried you. But now, do tell me, what do you think was the most daring thing you ever did?'

'Well,' said Martin, 'you'll understand I can only tell you things which were found out or to which I confessed.

Otherwise, the Statute of Limitations not running for the benefit of criminals, I might find myself in a difficulty.'

'Of course. I'm not trying to trap you into an admission. I shouldn't succeed anyway.'

'Now let me think,' said Martin. 'I think the most amusing thing I ever did was to adjourn someone else's case over the Long Vacation.'

'What d'you mean by that?'

'I'll explain. There was an action on between two firms. We'll call them Smith and Brown. Both of them had subpoenaed me to give evidence. The truth of the matter was that I had defrauded each of them, and although they both knew I was concerned, they sued each other because they didn't realise I'd duped them both. There was only about a couple of thousand pounds involved, which in those days wasn't very much to me. However, I hadn't got it at the time. If I had I'd have paid them out.'

'Why?'

'Well, I knew that, if I went into the witness box, my fraud would be discovered, the papers would be sent to the Director of Public Prosecutions, and I should be on my way to the Old Bailey again. Given a bit of time I could probably get the £2,000 and all would be well. People very rarely prosecute for fraud if they get their money. I used to have a reserve fund for this purpose. Unfortunately, however, at the time it was down to practically nothing. The case between Smith and Brown had started in December and I had hoped that it wouldn't be tried until the following October. However, it started to creep up in the list, and by July 24th it was quite plain that, unless something were done, it would be bound to come on that term. July 31st (which is normally the last day of term) was a Sunday, and so the last effective day was Friday the 29th. *Smith v Brown* was bound to come on by the 28th. It was not a very long case, but it would have taken at least two days. I knew on July 22nd that it was not in Monday's list. That meant it would be on or after the 26th. Now, I had by this time had a good deal of experience of the Law Courts. I had appeared several times as a litigant, sometimes in person, sometimes represented, and I knew the way things happened there. I decided that something drastic must be done. I went to a theatrical costumiers and hired a barrister's outfit, you know, wig, bands and gown. I put them in a suitcase and went to the Law Courts. I don't suppose you know, but every day a judge deals with applications to adjourn cases or take them out of the list. I had noticed the way these applications were made and how they were dealt with. At the proper time I went into a lavatory with my suitcase and came out of it duly robed as a barrister. I put my suitcase on a bench in the corridor. It was an old one and unlikely to be stolen in the ten minutes or so during which it was left. I went into the Court where Mr Justice Briggs was about to hear applications. I gave my name to the associate. I gave it as Dempster. I may add that, for safety's sake, I had put on a small false moustache before I went to the costumiers. I gave the associate the name of the case and its number in the list and I told him that no one was appearing on the other side. There was a risk, of course that one or other of the counsel engaged in the case would happen to be present, but I knew them by sight and I was glad to see that they were not. In due course I stepped into the barristers' row, and when everyone else had finished, I got up and requested his Lordship's permission to mention the case of *Smith v Brown*.

' "Yes, Mr Dempster," said the judge, looking at the little piece of paper on which my name was. He had, of course, never heard of me or even seen me before, but he was quite used to that, and they don't turn up your name in the Law List just because they've never heard of you. If you appear properly robed you will be accepted as a genuine barrister. Even if they did look in the Law List, you might have been called too late for your name to have been inserted. So I was quite safe as far as that was concerned.

' "My Lord," I said, "I appear in that case for the plaintiff on behalf of my learned friend Mr Smithers. My learned friend Mr Carter appears for the defendant. I have seen him and he consents to this application but is unfortunately unable to be here."

' "What is the application?" asks the judge.

' "My Lord, it is an application to stand the case out of the list until next term on the ground of the sudden and serious illness of one of the plaintiff's essential witnesses. I have a doctor's certificate which I will hand up to your Lordship."

'I handed up a piece of paper with a stamped address on it. I had obtained it as a sample and I have no idea who lived there. On it I had written with reasonable illegibility that I certified that Mr Harold Cartwright was suffering from a severe attack of appendicitis requiring immediate operation, and that, assuming the operation were successful, he would not be fit to give evidence for at least six weeks. I signed the certificate in the first name that I could think of (other than my own) and added MRCS, LRCP, after it.

' "You say that Mr Carter consents to this application?" said the judge.

' "Yes, my Lord. He is on his feet before the Lord Chief Justice. He said he would come if he could."

' "He might have sent someone instead," said the judge, "but very well. The case will stand out of the list until next term."

'I thanked his Lordship, bowed, withdrew, found my suitcase, went back to the lavatory, disrobed and emerged again. I returned the outfit to the costumiers and shortly afterwards removed my moustache. A moustache is comparatively rare at the Bar and I thought it possible that, when later on the matter arose for investigation, the associate and possibly the judge also would remember that the application was made by someone with a moustache. The next day the case was not in the list. The solicitors and counsel on each side were no doubt a little surprised, but they assumed that it had been passed over for some reason and would be in the next day. I was lucky in that there were no additions to the list for Wednesday, though probably, even if they had started to unravel the matter then, it would have been too late. Both parties must naturally have assumed that the case would be in on Thursday, and when it was not, things must have started to happen. Probably counsel's clerk went over to the office of the chief associate to know what had happened. He would at once have been told that the case had been adjourned as the result of an application. I expect he went back to chambers and telephoned the solicitors and told them. This is the sort of dialogue I imagine.

' "But I never instructed you to apply for an adjournment."

' "I didn't say you did. You must have instructed someone else."

' "Now don't be ridiculous. Mr Smithers is doing the case for us. They must have mixed it up with another case. Go back and see."

'I expect the clerk went back.

' "You must have made a mistake in *Smith v Brown*," he will have said. "There's been no application."

' "No application? I tell you I was there myself and heard it."

' "We had no instructions to apply. Mr Smithers certainly wasn't there."

' "I didn't say he was. Here you are; it was a man called Dempster. Said he appeared for Smithers."

' "That's impossible. We haven't anyone in chambers called Dempster."

' "Now, look here, I've got a great deal to do. I can't help the way you do your work or who you get to appear for Mr Smithers. The application was made, a medical certificate produced, and the case was adjourned. That's all."

'Counsel's clerk, somewhat mystified but quite satisfied that he himself was in no way to blame, no doubt went straight back to chambers to see his principal, Mr Smithers.

' "Would you go over and see him, please, sir," I expect he said.

' "I'll speak to the solicitors first and to Carter," says Mr Smithers.

'Having fortified himself with their denials of any knowledge of the matter, Mr Smithers goes over to see the chief associate.

' "Sorry to worry you," he says, "but it's about *Smith v Brown*."

'The chief associate is always very helpful to counsel, but he is a busy man.

' "I'm fed to the teeth with *Smith and Brown*," he says. "It's been adjourned. I told your clerk so."

' " I can't understand it. Who applied?"

' "Dempster, on a doctor's certificate."

' "Who's Dempster?"

' "You should know."

' "Well, I don't. Never heard of him. Do you know him?"

' "No, I don't, as a matter of fact."

' "Let's see where his chambers are."

'They probably looked first of all in the telephone book. No Dempster in the Temple. Then in the Law List. No Dempster. Must only just have been called, they say. By the time they had satisfied themselves that the thing was a complete mystery, it was, of course, far too late for the case to be heard. The whole affair remained, for them, a mystery, until some years later when I was convicted of another offence, and, in case of accidents, asked for the other matter to be taken into consideration. It raised quite a sensation at the time. At first no one believed that it could be done, but they checked up on it eventually. I must say I should have liked to have been present at some of the interviews with the chief associate.'

'Thank you very much,' said the journalist. 'I can certainly use that. Now what about something the other way? Something that didn't come off?'

'Well, I know the time I was most annoyed. Chiefly with myself, though. It was a bad mistake to have made, but I was a bit down at the time and I quite overlooked the point. Oh, I was angry, I can tell you. As I've said, it was at a time when things weren't too good and I was on the lookout for anything. But it was very stupid of me. I was walking along one day when I saw a poor chap skid on a bicycle, crash into a lamp post, and kill himself. It was no one's fault, but I took the precaution of taking the number of a car which was passing at the time. As I told you, in my job you've got to be on the lookout all the while. Well, I did what I could for him, and eventually a crowd and a policeman came along. They called the ambulance and took him to hospital, but it soon had to be the mortuary.

214

We all told the policeman that we hadn't seen anything, but I was careful to add that a man had said to me that he'd seen it but that he couldn't stop and would call at a police station later and tell them about it. I then ferreted around among my more doubtful acquaintances, until I found a chap who hadn't been inside, and, as far as I could tell, had nothing against him; nothing known against him, that is. I got him to agree to my plan and then went off to see the relatives. I told them that, if they'd agree to share the damages with me, I'd get them a large sum. They did agree. My acquaintance then went to the police station and told them how a car with the number I'd given him had just touched the cycle and sent it into a skid. It didn't seem to be a case for a prosecution, but, of course, there was an inquest. They traced the driver, who had to admit that he was there just about that time, but who, of course, denied having touched any cyclist. My friend swore he had. The verdict was accidental death. I then instructed solicitors on behalf of the relatives and they made a claim on the driver, who naturally referred the matter to his insurance company. Now, look at it from the insurance company's point of view. Here's an admitted accident, the insured was there at the time, and an apparently independent witness says that he just touched the cyclist. Which is the more likely, that the driver didn't notice just touching him or that the independent witness is inventing the story? Obviously the former. From the company's point of view a judge would appear almost bound to decide in favour of the relatives. Of course, if they'd known I had anything to do with it, it would have been different, but apart from getting the solicitors to act, I kept well out of the way. The long and the short of it was that the insurance company paid up. £3,000 they paid.

And when I went for my share what do you think happened?

' "Have a drink," they say, "we're ever so grateful to you."

' "Here's luck," I said, not realising how much out of it I was.

'I didn't mention the money at first and neither did they. The time came when we'd run short of things to say to one another, and it was fairly clear that they were expecting me to go. So I had to begin.

' "Well," I said, "if you'll just let me have my little cheque, I'll be off."

' "Oh," they said, "we were afraid you'd say that."

' "Afraid?" I said. "You agreed to give me half the damages, didn't you?"

' "That's right," they said.

' "Well, let's have it then, please."

' "We'd like to," they said.

' "I'm not stopping you," I said. "On the contrary."

' "Perhaps *you'd* be able to explain better."

' "What on earth do you mean?" I asked. I was getting anxious and angry by this time. "Me explain? You're the people to explain. Where's my money?"

' "We couldn't get it," they said. "We tried."

' "Now don't be silly," I said. "You've had £3,000 haven't you?"

' "Well, we have and we haven't, you might say."

' "Look here," I said, "this isn't a quiz. I'm in a hurry and don't want to play games. Where's my money?"

' "In court," they said.

'The penny dropped. Damages of this kind have to be paid into court for the benefit of the widow and children and can only be paid out on application to the court, which has to safeguard the interests of the parties concerned. I must have gone white, because they offered me a chair and another drink.

' "We tried to get it," they said.

' "You tried to get it?" I asked faintly.

' "Yes," they said, "we went to the County Court Judge and said we'd agreed to give you half the damages and asked him for the money."

'I paused for a moment to get the full flavour.

' "Did you – did you give him my name?" I asked eventually.

' "Oh yes," they said, "but it didn't make any difference. He just wrote it down, that's all, and said that we couldn't have any of the money for the moment. Perhaps if you went to him and explained he might let you have it."

'Well, you can see what's going to happen. Not only did I get nothing out of it, but eventually I got two years into the bargain. The County Court Judge had enquiries made, and when the police saw my name they went into the matter closely. They picked up my friend and questioned him. Of course, he was a fool to let them. The number of people who give themselves away, because they don't know their legal rights, is dreadful. The police can ask you questions if they like, but you're not bound to answer them, let alone go to the police station to do so. My friend admitted everything and we were both arrested. They told my friend to plead guilty and give evidence against me, and said that he wouldn't be sent to prison if he did. So he agreed. They were wrong about his not going to prison, though I must say they tried to keep their promise. To have heard the nice things the inspector said about him, you'd have thought he was counsel appearing on his behalf, but the judge was in the way. My friend got six months. Serve him right. Of course, the poor wretched people I'd tried to help had to give all the money back, but a newspaper raised a fund for them and they got £500 instead. I kicked myself over that, I can tell you. It annoys me even now. I ought to have thought of it. Don't talk to me about paying money into court. It ought to be abolished.'

'Well, I can use that, too, thank you very much,' said the journalist. 'Now what about Mrs Painswick? How have you found things?'

'Well, I can't pretend it isn't nice to have him back for good, but I managed all right, and then for some time I had Charlie to keep me company.'

'Charlie – a son, I suppose?'

'Yes, that's right.'

'I didn't know you had any children.'

'Oh, yes – just the one. We got him to change his name. You know. Thought it might help.'

'And where's he these days?'

'Well, today, as a matter of fact, he's at the Old Bailey.'

'The Old Bailey? Oh dear, oh dear, I'm so sorry. I wouldn't have asked you if I'd known. Must take after his father, I'm afraid.'

'After his father?' said Martin. 'Not a bit of it. After his grandfather. He's a judge.'

HENRY CECIL

ACCORDING TO THE EVIDENCE

Alec Morland is on trial for murder. He has tried to remedy the ineffectiveness of the law by taking matters into his own hands. Unfortunately for him, his alleged crime was not committed in immediate defence of others or of himself. In this fascinating murder trial you will not find out until the very end just how the law will interpret his actions. Will his defence be accepted or does a different fate await him?

THE ASKING PRICE

Ronald Holbrook is a fifty-seven-year-old bachelor who has lived in the same house for twenty years. Jane Doughty, the daughter of his next-door neighbours, is seventeen. She suddenly decides she is in love with Ronald and wants to marry him. Everyone is amused at first but then events take a disturbingly sinister turn and Ronald finds himself enmeshed in a potentially tragic situation.

'The secret of Mr Cecil's success lies in continuing to do superbly what everyone now knows he can do well.'
– *The Sunday Times*

HENRY CECIL

BRIEF TALES FROM THE BENCH

What does it feel like to be a Judge? Read these stories and you can almost feel you are looking at proceedings from the lofty position of the Bench.

With a collection of eccentric and amusing characters, Henry Cecil brings to life the trials in a County Court and exposes the complex and often contradictory workings of the English legal system.

'Immensely readable. His stories rely above all on one quality – an extraordinary, an arresting, a really staggering ingenuity.'
– *New Statesman*

BROTHERS IN LAW

Roger Thursby, aged twenty-four, is called to the bar. He is young, inexperienced and his love life is complicated. He blunders his way through a succession of comic adventures including his calamitous debut at the bar.

His career takes an upward turn when he is chosen to defend the caddish Alfred Green at the Old Bailey. In this first Roger Thursby novel Henry Cecil satirizes the legal profession with his usual wit and insight.

'Uproariously funny.' – *The Times*

'Full of charm and humour. I think it is the best Henry Cecil yet.' – P G Wodehouse

Henry Cecil

Hunt the Slipper

Harriet and Graham have been happily married for twenty years. One day Graham fails to return home and Harriet begins to realise she has been abandoned. This feeling is strengthened when she starts to receive monthly payments from an untraceable source. After five years on her own Harriet begins to see another man and divorces Graham on the grounds of his desertion. Then one evening Harriet returns home to find Graham sitting in a chair, casually reading a book. Her initial relief turns to anger and then to fear when she realises that if Graham's story is true, she may never trust his sanity again. This complex comedy thriller will grip your attention to the very last page.

Sober as a Judge

Roger Thursby, the hero of *Brothers in Law* and *Friends at Court*, continues his career as a High Court judge. He presides over a series of unusual cases, including a professional debtor and an action about a consignment of oranges which turned to juice before delivery. There is a delightful succession of eccentric witnesses as the reader views proceedings from the Bench.

'The author's gift for brilliant characterisation makes this a book that will delight lawyers and laymen as much as did its predecessors.' – *The Daily Telegraph*

Made in the USA
Middletown, DE
27 August 2019